WHEN DEATH KNOCKS

S.C. STOKES

PRESCIENT PUBLISHING

CONTENTS

CHAPTER 1

At that moment, one maniacal wizard plotted the destruction and misery of millions of souls. New York City, and everyone in it was in imminent danger. With countless lives hanging in the balance, Kasey couldn't help but think of those that had already been lost.

The assembly around Kasey fell silent as a single figure rose to his feet. His brief walk from his chair to the podium was made in measured strides. The man was dressed in his navy-blue NYPD dress uniform, from the toe of his brightly polished shoes to the embroidered tip of his police cover. The three gold stars embroidered into his lapel, designated him as the chief of one of New York City's many police precincts.

To Kasey, he was more than just a police chief. He was her chief. He had taken a chance on her, even though her world had been falling apart. There were few people in New York City willing to stand up to the political machine of the Ainsleys and their money. West had not yielded an inch. He had sheltered her from the storm.

Kasey was close enough that she could see his puffy eyes and his red tinged nose. Her heart broke knowing what the chief had endured these past few days. She watched as his lip quivered ever so slightly.

Reaching the podium, the chief straightened, and drew in a deep breath. The gray sprinkled through his mustache and hair only served to highlight his distinguished appearance. Chief West was a highly decorated officer and a pillar of the community. Few were the foes brave or foolish enough to cross his path. The chief stood, silently waiting at the podium. The improvised stage had been hastily erected in the center of Madison Square Garden.

The Garden had hosted countless events over its illustrious lifetime. From charity galas, to sporting matches to rock concerts. John Lennon, Patrick Ewing, and Elton John, Madison Square Garden had seen them all. Several times it had even hosted the NBA finals and the Stanley cup finals simultaneously. Cheering fans were known to drown the immense arena in a cacophony of revelry as they cheered their home-town heroes to glory.

Every seat was filled today, but no one was cheering. The entire arena was melancholy. Kasey waited in sobering silence for the Chief to begin.

His gaze scanned across the caskets lining the space before the stage. Eighteen caskets, each adorned with a flag of the United States of America, the country its officers had served so valiantly.

The normally steely-eyed chief reached up and swept a tear from his eye.

Taking a deep breath, he began, "As you are aware, I am Jonathan West, Chief of the NYPD's Ninth District. The Fighting Ninth,"

His anguish was clearly visible, from the wrinkled corners of his eyes to his tightly drawn upper lip.

"You have all heard and seen the senseless violence that befell our precinct last week. These caskets that you see before you today hold the bodies of our valiant men and women, who gave their lives in defense of this city, in defense of you. These eighteen brave men and women made the greatest sacrifice one can make. They did so for you, and for me. They did so, so that this city would be a safer place for each of us. For our families. Each and every one of them were an officer worthy of the uniform which they wore proudly. We mourn them as a precinct, as a city, and as a nation. We mourn them as our family."

Kasey felt tears well up in her eyes as she thought of her fallen colleagues.

The chief continued. "It is my intention that a monument will be erected in the lobby of the Ninth Precinct, where their badges will remain as a memorial of their courage, heroism, and sacrifice. Let all who come to that place, now and forevermore, know that they laid down their lives for their country.

"As for the cowardly organization who perpetrated this act of senseless violence, I am here to raise the warning voice."

Kasey's heart skipped a beat.

Chief West grasped the podium with both hands. "You are here in our city, in our home. The NYPD will not be bullied nor beaten into submission. We will fight you with every fiber of our being and with every breath in our body. We will hunt you down and you will answer for your crimes. With you all as my witness, I swear that today, just as in days past, that we will stand in defense of our people and our city. New York will never give in. It will never surrender, and neither will we. Flee while you still can. Today we bury our fallen and tomorrow we're coming for you. You may have begun this bloodshed, but we will end it and you."

He straightened to his full height and drew a deep breath. "Would you all please stand, as the Honor guards carry our officers to the vehicles that will bear them to their final resting place. Internment services will be directed by the families of these brave men and women. We ask that you respect their wishes and that you wait for them to depart the building before you attempt to return home.

"My brave officers of the Fighting Ninth, rest in peace, you might be gone but you'll never be forgotten."

Stepping to the side of the pulpit, Chief West snapped a salute. The assembly rose to its feet. The Honor guard consisting of the surviving officers of the Fighting Ninth took their places beside the caskets. As one they raised the caskets and bore them from the arena.

As the funeral procession filed from the arena, the deep resonating notes of bagpipes filled the stadium. The families of the fallen officers wept openly as each soulful chord of Amazing Grace echoed through the vast stadium.

Kasey's heart went out to the Chief, and to her fallen comrades. The attack on the precinct had been swift and brutal. Together with Bishop and Vida she had only narrowly escaped death herself. What Chief West and the other officers of the Ninth Precinct didn't know, was the true reason behind the attack.

The Shinigami and their thuggish acolytes had attacked the precinct in a misguided attempt to rescue one of their own, Mina, who had died while Kasey and Bishop had been trying to arrest her. Mina had been run down by a taxi and taken to the Ninth Precinct for her autopsy.

Two more had died during the attack on the precinct, along with more than a dozen acolytes they had brought with them.

The Shinigami were a cabal of Japanese wizards bent on destruction. The Shinigami traversed the world inflicting misery and devastation in order to study the forbidden art of necromancy. Obsessed with death and the ability to live forever, the Shinigami pursued their goal with single-minded intent. At home in Japan, the Shinigami were feared as the harbingers of death. Now the Shinigami had come to New York. What had brought them to the city, was not entirely clear, but Kasey's gut told her there was a connection with the coming attack on the city. Ever since she was a child, she had been afflicted with visions of the attack. The city being devastated by explosions as arcane forces tore the city apart. Recent events had led her to believe the attack was imminent. The Shinigami's arrival certainly heralded ill tidings for the city.

Fortunately for New York, Kasey knew it was coming and she was doing everything in her power to stop it.

Of the four Shinigami, three of them were now dead. Only one remained: The Master.

The same Master who had hired Danilo Lelac to kill her. He was also behind the plot to destroy the city. Unfortunately, the Shinigami possessed the means to alter their appearance with magic. As far as Kasey knew, the Master could be anyone. Searching for one maniacal wizard in a city of millions was a monumental task. One that she needed to begin at once.

She watched as the arena around her emptied. As much as she longed to mourn her fallen comrades, time was not a luxury she could afford. If she could not find and thwart the organization behind the attack on New York, there would be many more tears. Everyone in the city was in danger.

She left her seat and followed the throng of people moving toward the exit.

The assembly wound their way out of the stadium. Many of the surrounding streets had been closed to allow the funerary procession swift passage through the city. Police lined the streets, forming a solemn guard of Honor. While the procession moved south, Kasey turned north. Making her way to 7th Avenue, Kasey quickened her pace.

There was little point in heading back to the Ninth Precinct. Repairs were still underway on the station, particularly the precinct's morgue. In an effort to save Vida's life, Bishop and Kasey had barricaded themselves inside the morgue and made their last stand. The arcane conflict that had ensued had destroyed the morgue's examination facilities, along with most of its equipment. What little remained was certainly not fit to perform any form of autopsy. In the meantime, most of the Fighting Ninth's forensic work was being attended to by the nearby 13th Precinct, leaving Kasey free to run down leads on the Shinigami's plot to destroy the city.

Truth be told, Kasey was still feeling guilty about bringing the Shinigami's wrath down on the Ninth Precinct. If she'd known the danger that they posed, she would have considered a different course of action.

Too late for regrets now. I can't change the past, only the future.

She passed Times Square and turned down West 47th Street. With the Shinigami Master in hiding, she wanted to investigate the only other aspect of the attack she had uncovered: 432 Park Avenue.

Upon completion, the towering skyscraper would be one of the tallest residential buildings in the world. In New York City, the only building taller was One World Trade Center. 432 Park Avenue was a 1396-foot-tall complex, and an architectural masterpiece. The slender structure reached for the heavens, offering panoramic views of the New York City skyline. From the Hudson to the East River, Westchester to Brooklyn and from Central Park to the Atlantic Ocean, there wasn't an apartment in the city that could compete with its impressive views.

Kasey's interest in the building stemmed from a vision she had witnessed. In one of her visions, she had stood on its observation deck watching the attack on New York City unfold below. In spite of its towering majesty, 432 Park Avenue had stood completely unscathed as the city crumbled around it. I want to know why.

Something about the building made it immune to the arcane assault. If she could work out what that was, there was a chance she could use the knowledge to save the rest of the city. It was a long shot, but it was the only lead she had.

As she turned up Park Avenue, the construction site came into view. The building already dwarfed those around it. A crane sat perched precariously atop the rising structure. From her place on the city street it looked minuscule, but she knew it was simply a matter of perspective. The crane itself was likely several stories tall and would rise with the structure until it was completed.

432 Park Avenue wasn't due for completion for several months, but already almost eighty percent of the building's luxury apartments had been pre-purchased. An apartment at

this end of town would have taken several lifetimes for Kasey to afford on her Medical Examiner's salary.

No harm in taking a look while I'm here though. A little window shopping never hurt anyone.

As she approached the construction site, she considered her options.

More than once, she had used her magic to imitate a government agency ID to further her investigations. Only weeks ago, she'd impersonated a police officer while investigating the serial killer Danilo Lelac. On that particular excursion, she'd almost been eaten by a Werewolf and ended up being thrown through a glass window. If it wasn't for Bishop's arrival, she might have been killed. As it was, her unexplainable presence at the site of a murder had resulted in her spending the night in holding.

She slowed her pace so that she could observe the site. The building had been sealed off with temporary fencing, and a singular checkpoint controlled the only entrance to the construction yard. Two security guards manned the booth. Everyone entering the site was having their ID checked.

I need a look at one of those tags.

Kasey watched as a pair of tradesmen left the site and ambled over to a street cart. She quickened her pace and stepped into line behind them. The shorter of the two, a rotund bearded man, pointed down the street to where a parking inspector was printing a ticket. The inspector was standing next to a silver Mercedes. Clearly it had overstayed its meter. The inspector lifted the printed ticket with a flourish and slid it under the vehicles windscreen wiper. The inspector smiled and continued down the street.

Whoever the vehicle belonged to, the workers were taking great pleasure in its owner's unwelcome gift.

Kasey glanced down. The workers' ID cards were clipped to their tool belts. Kasey sized up the workers. The bearded man's companion was a well-toned man in his early thirties with a shaved head. His ID was only inches from Kasey.

She inched a little closer, readying herself to lift the ID. She would need it so that she could duplicate its design. As she reached for the ID, a commotion at the gates drew her eye.

A balding middle-aged man was passing through the checkpoint as he left the site, all the while shouting into his smart phone. His furious tone may have drawn Kasey's attention, but it was his attire that kept it. He was wearing a suit in a construction yard and looking distinctly out of place. The security guards simply opened the gate to let him through. Kasey couldn't help but notice, he wore no ID whatsoever.

As he left the site, Kasey strained to overhear his conversation.

"You tell him that if his crew isn't on site tomorrow at seven am, we'll be suing him for breach of contract. By the time I'm through with him, he won't so much as change a washer in New York City ever again."

The two workers in front of her snickered as the man's pasty complexion slowly turned scarlet. He looked as though he might burst a blood vessel at any moment.

Kasey knew she needed more information. Tapping the bearded tradesman on the shoulder, she asked, "Who's that piece of work?"

The tradesman turned, one eyebrow raised. "You don't know Sal Langstrode?"

"If I did, I wouldn't be asking now, would I?" Kasey replied sharply. "Who is he?"

"Easy tiger," the bald tradesman replied as he eyed Kasey up and down.

Kasey clenched her fists but forced herself to take a deep breath.

"He owns the place." The worker continued pointing to the temporary fence.

Kasey followed his gesture and noticed the fence was covered in branding. The most prominent sign read, 'Langstrode Developments - Shaping the Skyline of New York since 1935.'

Just the man I need. He'll know everything there is to know about this monstrosity.

She stepped out of line and approached the developer.

"You're welcome," The tradesman called after her.

She simply waved as if shooing a bothersome fly. She couldn't get away from him quick enough.

Langstrode hung up his phone and shoved it into his pocket. Kasey followed him as he stormed to his car: the silver Mercedes that had just been ticketed by the parking inspector.

Langstrode drew his keys out of his pocket and pressed the button. The Mercedes' lights flickered once, and the doors unlocked. As he reached the car, he spotted the slip of paper under the wiper.

"What the...?" he muttered as he pulled out the slip. His face contorted. "Again? You have to be kidding me."

He tore the tiny slip of paper in half. Then, he continued to scrunch and tear the parking fine until he'd reduced it to confetti before casting it away.

"I'll give you a fine," he mumbled as he reached for the door. Kasey hesitated. Not that she feared the developer's petulant temper, but more out of concern for what she might do to him, should he lose it. She was on thin ice after the incident with John Ainsley.

Seizing the moment, she stepped forward. "Mr. Langstrode. Can I have a moment."

The developer didn't bother to look at her. He simply barked over his shoulder as he reached for the door, "Get lost. I'm in a hurry."

She was not deterred. She simply stepped around him and blocked the door with her hip, preventing him from opening it.

"What do you think you are doing?" he demanded.

She was about to answer when the mist descended, clouding her sight completely.

Breathing deeply, she welcomed the vision.

CHAPTER 2

When the mist cleared, Kasey found herself standing in the middle of a construction site. The floor's framework had been completed but its internal walls and windows were yet to be installed. The view of New York's skyline from this height would have been breathtaking if not for the two thugs barreling toward her.

The men may have been wearing suits, but there was no mistaking their intent. Tight shirts and no ties, the men were hired muscle and they were almost on top of her.

Before she could react, the nearest thug grabbed her arm. He was a brawny mountain of a man with a shaved head and surprisingly well trimmed mustache. Kasey looked down and realized it wasn't her arm. It was in a suit, and she had a policy against pantsuits.

She knew at once she was experiencing the vision from someone else's perspective.

Not again.

The second thug grabbed her other arm. Kasey felt herself being lifted off her feet.

"What the hell is going on here?" a voice shouted. It was a man's voice. It only took Kasey a moment to place it. She'd just heard it moments ago, as he had railed down the phone at an unexpected delay.

Langstrode.

"Do you know who I am? I own this building! Put me down now and I won't press charges."

The man with the well-trimmed mustache chuckled. "Oh, we'll put you down alright. Don't be in a hurry, old man."

"Old man?" Kasey could feel Langstrode struggling against the thugs but with his feet in the air, he couldn't get any traction.

"Sal, Sal, Sal," a voice began, it didn't appear to be either of the thugs speaking.

The newcomer's voice was unfamiliar. It was quiet but unyielding.

Langstrode's head spun about as he searched for the source of the voice.

"Who is that? Do I know you?" Langstrode's voice wavered. It was becoming clear that the thug's presence was not a case of mistaken identity. They were here for him.

"No, Sal. You don't know me, but you don't need to," the voice said.

This time, Kasey was able to get a fix on it. Several drop cloths obscured one corner of the room. The voice was coming from behind the sheets.

Are you kidding me? Kasey seethed internally. Whoever it was, they were cautious.

"Who are you? I can pay you. I have money," Langstrode stammered.

The floor was quiet but for Langstrode's struggling against the thugs. When no response was forthcoming, he tried again.

"Name your price. Have these monkeys put me down. I'll get you anything you want." Langstrode's voice trembled as he spoke.

"I know you will, Sal. I know you will. Unfortunately, the die is already cast, Sal. There is no changing your fate."

Langstrode was sweating, his palms clammy and shaking with every breath.

"Whatever you're being paid, I can double it," Langstrode begged.

"That won't be necessary, Sal. There's only one thing I need from you now."

"What's that?"

"I need you to step outside." The voice chuckled. "Boys, see him out."

"Outside? Wait, no!" Langstrode's voice cracked as his protestations deteriorated into incoherent rambling.

He thrashed violently against the thugs, but he was outmatched.

Kasey felt helpless as Langstrode was hoisted toward the edge of the building. Reaching the ledge, the pair shuffled onto the scaffolding surrounding it. They hefted Langstrode like he was nothing. Langstrode arced up and over the steel framework. Kasey sucked in a deep breath as she got a breathtaking view of New York City, before she began plummeting to the Earth.

Her stomach flipped as Langstrode free fell through the air. Langstrode screams were interrupted by two gunshots splitting the night air.

As the ground rushed toward her, Kasey began to squirm internally.

This is going to suck...

Out of nowhere, the mist descended, cutting off her vision.

Standing near his car, Sal Langstrode stared at Kasey.

"What are you waiting for?" he said. "Get out of my way."

"In a moment. First, I want to know why someone wants you dead."

Langstrode stopped. His brown eyes were wide, and his lower jaw slowly sank open. He was uncharacteristically speechless.

"I said, who would want to kill you?" Kasey asked, gripping the top of the door.

"What's it to you?" Sal asked. "Who are you, anyway?"

Kasey glanced down and realized she wasn't wearing her NYPD windbreaker. To Langstrode, she must've come across as a crazy random person off the street.

She reached into her pocket and drew out her ID. "My apologies, Mr. Langstrode. I'm Kasey Chase and I'm with the NYPD."

Seizing the opportunity to find out more about her vision, she raised her ID so Langstrode could get a good look at it. Bishop had asked the Department to issue her one, to avoid any further misunderstandings at crime scenes.

Sal's left eyebrow arched suspiciously as he leaned closer to inspect the ID. "This says Crime Scene Technician, not police officer. Shouldn't a real detective be working this lead? Why would the department send someone like you to speak with me?"

Kasey bit her tongue.

That arrogant little... I have half a mind to let them throw him off the building.

Drawing on all the self-restraint she could muster, Kasey answered him. "You are right, Sal, normally you would have a detective here asking you exactly the same questions. Unfortunately for you, sixteen of our officers were gunned down last week. The funerals are taking place today and we are a little short staffed. Everyone else that might be here running down this lead must have heard of your rosy disposition because they would all rather be at the funeral. I'm starting to see why."

Sal's face began to redden.

Kasey pressed on. "We received a tip that a contract had been taken out on your life. While we believe it may be credible, today is a day of mourning for the Ninth Precinct. They won't be diverting resources from honoring our fallen officers, to protecting the life of a snotty Upper East side developer."

Angry creases began to form on his forehead.

Before he could open his mouth, Kasey continued, "So, Sal, today, I'm the best you've got. Either talk to me or don't. That's your choice. Any information you can give us that will help us identify and neutralize the threat against your life will clearly be in your best interest. Or keep being a jackass if you wish. It's your life. If you don't care about it, why should we?"

Langstrode let go of the door handle and stepped right up to Kasey. "Listen, here, you wretched little girl. I'm Sal Langstrode. My vision has shaped this city. I have built more buildings in this city than any other man alive. From whining tenants, to crooked cops and vicious mobsters, I have been cussed at, beaten, blackmailed, extorted, and mugged twice. If you think you can scare me, you are sadly mistaken."

Kasey didn't blink. Her eyes bored straight into his. "Sal, I'm only going to tell you this once. Back off. Back off, or I will make everything you have suffered seem like a picnic. I don't care how much money you have. If you don't get out of my face, you are going to want to die.

"Besides, what don't you get? I am here to help you. We received a credible threat on your life. Unfortunately, our precinct couldn't spare any resources today. So rather than leave you alone and hope for the best, my partner sent me. Clearly, she had no idea how cantankerous and irritating you are. Otherwise, she might have just left you to your fate. This is New York City, after all. You're not the only man who might die today."

Her defiance and determination seemed to hit the mark. Langstrode backed off and let go of the door. Turning to face Kasey, he leaned back against the car and sighed heavily.

"So, what do you know?" he asked. "You said someone is out to kill me. What are we looking at?"

Kasey raced to improvise a story. Telling him she had seen a vision of him being thrown off his own building would not have the result she was seeking. He was more likely to consider her crazy and laugh in her face before getting in his expensive car driving away. She needed another angle.

"One of our criminal informants overheard a contract being put on your life. They couldn't get close enough to hear the details, but the tip came in last night. Our informant is credible. His information has led to at least three other arrests in the last two months. We have every reason to believe the threat to your life is both real, and imminent."

Sal nodded. "Do we have any idea who was hired? What can I expect?"

Kasey shook her head. "I'm sorry, all our informant heard was your name and the sum of one hundred thousand dollars being discussed. It's likely that the man he overheard was simply the middleman. We have no way of knowing exactly who is after you. That's why I'm here."

Langstrode's face crinkled up. "What? To give me nothing and scare the hell out of me?"

"No," Kasey said. "To find out who might want you dead. We need your help narrowing the field. Right now, based on everything I know about you, it seems like most of New York city wants you dead. I can hardly blame them. I've only known you for five minutes and already I'm thinking a hundred grand? I'll do it for free. It would be an act of community service."

He shook his head in disbelief. "A hundred grand. What a joke. I'd barely get out of bed for that. It's hard to believe someone would be willing to risk life in prison for so little."

"You don't come down from the ivory tower very often, do you, Sal? This is New York City. There are plenty of people here who would kill you for that expensive watch you're wearing. The hundred thousand is plenty, trust me. I see the crime scenes every day. People have done a lot more for a lot less. Now I need you to stop beating around the bush and give me what we need to save your life."

He folded his arms across his chest. "Oh, yeah? What's that?"

Kasey pulled out her phone and hit record. "Tell me anyone you can think of who might want you dead."

"It's a bit of a list," he admitted reluctantly. "It could take some time."

She nodded. "Why do you think I'm recording it, and not writing it down?"

"You're a piece of work," he said.

"Yup, and you're an endangered species. Now, start at the top. You can start with whoever you were shouting down the phone at earlier."

Sal took a deep breath. "That was nothing. Just one of my tradesmen who decided not to show up to work today. Apparently, they double booked us with another job in Queens. I mean Queens, come on, you're going to skip out on making history with this masterpiece so that you can fix some old woman's leaky pipes in Queens.

"What a joke. I was just suggesting he get his priorities in order. You don't need to worry about him, though. I pay him far too much for him to want to kill me. His plumbing business would just about go under if it wasn't for all the work I send his way."

Kasey nodded. "I see. So, you figure your plumber won't bite the hand that feeds him?"

"Exactly," Sal said. "He needs me if he wants to continue in the lifestyle he's become accustomed to."

She tapped her foot impatiently. "Right. If not the plumber, then who? You said you have your fair share of enemies. Who's on that list?"

He thought for a moment. "I have made my living, tearing down tired old buildings and replacing them with majestic masterpieces to enrich the city skyline. Unfortunately, the tired old buildings aren't entirely deserted."

Kasey sighed. "I suppose that is code for, I have to evict the poor and the helpless in order to grow my fortune. How often?"

"Every time I build a new building. They are never completely empty. There are always a few tenants hanging on. They need to be, well, encouraged to find a new place to live. Don't worry, we don't do anything illegal. We simply raise the rent until it is no longer viable for them to live there. This isn't the eighties and we only do what is legal, nothing more nothing less."

"Yes," Kasey replied raising an eyebrow, "you're a real Mother Theresa. We should see you get a sainthood."

"Hey," he replied, "I don't judge what you do. A man has to make a living you know."

She scoffed. "I'm sure you are barely making ends meet. I can see from that expensive car you are currently using as a chair. I may cut up dead people for a living, but I do it so that we can get killers off the street and get justice for the victim's families."

"I thought you're a crime scene technician?" Sal asked

"I'm multi-talented," she said. "My profession was originally a medical examiner. I spend a lot of my time in the morgue."

He looked her up and down. "Well, that explains a lot."

"What's that supposed to mean?" Kasey demanded flicking her hair out of her face.

He chuckled. "I just figured there had to be a reason for your staggering social skills."

"Coming from the man everyone wants dead, I'll take that as a compliment. Now keep going, Sal. If you die, there is every chance you will end up on my table, and I really don't want any more work."

"Charming," he replied shifting his weight from one foot to the other.

"Back to the list. Who else wants to send you on a permanent vacation?"

"There are always rival developers, people who I've outbid or won projects off. There are other companies who were interested in this site. Park Avenue is premium real estate. Everyone involved in it is likely to make a fortune. Those who made promises to their investors and can't deliver are likely facing bankruptcy.

"One of them might want me dead, so that they can take over the project. With me out of the way, it would be easy enough to buy their way in with my investors."

Kasey nodded. Money was always a potential motive for murder. The voice in her vision certainly seemed to have a plan. Even Sal's offers to pay him off had fallen on deaf ears.

"Can you think of anyone in particular who would have the resources and inclination to want to oust you from the project?"

"There's probably a few," he replied. "Can I put together a list and send it over?"

"That many?" Kasey asked. "I don't envy you."

"I wouldn't want to miss anyone. It's in my best interest, after all, isn't it?"

"That it is," Kasey replied tapping the developer on the chest. "We've dealt with money and power as motives. What about sex?"

"Excuse me?" He was a little taken aback. Langstrode eyed Kasey's phone warily.

"Don't mind the phone. I'm not a divorce lawyer. Sex," she repeated, enjoying his discomfort. "Along with money and power, relationships or sex, is one of the foremost reasons for murder. Are you married, Sal?"

"Yes," he answered defensively.

"Happily?" she prodded, cocking her head to one side. "You don't have a mistress set up in one of these—what did you call them? —majestic masterpieces?"

"I'm not discussing that with you," he said.

"I'll take that as a yes," she answered.

"I didn't say that." He pushed off the car toward Kasey.

She raised a finger. "You didn't say no either. Which is as good as a yes. Does your wife know about it?"

"She has no idea," he answered. "Not that she'd care. I'm fairly sure she's having an affair of her own and it's not the first."

"Any idea who?" Kasey nudged. "After all, they could be involved."

"Not really. It will be her yoga instructor or her tennis coach or someone from the golf course. I never really cared to find out."

Kasey couldn't fathom his lack of interest in his wife's affair. "If you've never found out, how are you sure she is having one?"

Sal laughed openly. "Women my age don't tend to take up that many new sports without a reason. I'm sure one of her instructors is working overtime, if you know what I mean."

Kasey was incredulous. "You are unbelievable."

"Don't be indignant. Clearly you have no idea how expensive divorce can be on the Upper East side. Golf lessons are far cheaper, and you know what they say, happy wife, happy life."

Kasey shook her head.

Unbelievable.

"What about family? Have you got any kids?"

"Two. Martin and Alicia."

"How old are they?" Kasey asked

"Martin is twenty-six, Alicia is twenty-one. Surely you don't think my kids want me dead?"

Kasey's mouth tilted up into an ever so slight smile. "With you, I'm not willing to rule anything out. What can you tell me about them?"

"They are good kids. Well, some of my son's friends are real losers. They have led him astray and I'd love to get him away from their influence, but he is twenty-six. How much say does an old man really have? Some lessons he'll need to learn for himself."

A flashing warning symbol on her phone drew Kasey's eye. She checked it. The low battery signal was flickering.

Darn phones, these things can barely make it past lunch time before they need another charge.

She had to step up her questions, before the phone died.

"Right, shady friends, got it. We'll look into them. What about your daughter?"

"She is twenty-one and studying at New York's School of Interior Design. Seems to be doing well and has shown some interest in joining the family business."

Kasey's phone flickered for a moment before the screen went dead. She slid the phone back into a pocket.

"Thanks, Sal, that's given us something to go on. I'll pass my notes along to Detective Bishop. She'll be in touch as the investigation progresses."

"That's it?" Sal asked.

"For now," Kasey answered. "What, were you hoping that we could solve the case in one conversation?"

He shook his head. "I don't know, I guess I was hoping you would be able to give me some indication as to who is coming after me."

Kasey reached over and pat him on the back. "Me too, Sal. Unfortunately, it seems I drastically underestimated just how long the list of potential suspects might be. As far as I can see, you seem to irritate, alienate, or bankrupt everyone who comes in contact with you.

"So, when it comes to a list of people who might want you dead, the shortlist would be most of New York City, while a broader estimate would need to include most of the English-speaking world."

He stared her, frowning. "Thanks for being no help at all."

"My thoughts precisely," Kasey replied. "As I said, we'll be in touch. In the meantime, keep your head down and consider hiring some security."

She left him leaning on his car, speechless, and headed for the station.

As she made her way down the busy Manhattan streets, she couldn't help but wonder if the visions she had seen of Langstrode's imminent death were connected to the attack on the city.

Either way, I need to know more about him, and more about that building. I'm going to need help and I know just the man for the job.

CHAPTER 3

Kasey stood quietly in the battered remnants of the morgue. The Shinigami attack had devastated the Ninth Precinct, turning the busy police station into a battleground. The morgue was due for renovation, but the construction and restoration wouldn't begin for at least another week.

With the morgue out of commission, it became the perfect place for her to ponder on the events she had witnessed in her vision.

For once, she'd witnessed a vision of a murder while the victim was still alive. Now she was determined to do everything in her power to stop it.

Sal Langstrode may have been an arrogant jerk, but somehow, he and his residential tower were at the heart of the attack on the city. In her visions, Kasey had seen the city devastated. The earth-shattering explosions seemed to emanate out from 432 Park Avenue. The majestic structure remained unscathed while all around it, the city crumbled.

On the white board she had purloined from the bullpen, Kasey drew a circle and wrote 432 Park Avenue inside.

She drew a line out from the circle, then scribbled a stick figure and labeled it, Sal Langstrode. The man whose development lies at the heart of the attack on New York City. After drawing a long line out from the circle to the top of the board, she added another stick figure and labeled it, Master of the Shinigami. Next to it, she placed a large question mark.

While his comrades had been eliminated in the attack on the precinct, the Master of the Shinigami remained elusive. With his ability to alter his appearance with magic, there was no limit as to who he might be.

She drew a line out from the Shinigami Master and scribbled another figure on the board. Underneath it she wrote Danilo Lelac and then crossed out the figure.

So far in her struggle against the shadowy organization, she'd eliminated an assassin and three members of the Shinigami.

She took a step back and admired her handiwork.

Footsteps in the hall alerted her to the approach of others. She put the lid back on the marker and set it down on the tray of the white board.

She turned in time to see two familiar faces enter the morgue: Bishop and Vida.

"What's all this?" Bishop asked, pointing to the white board.

Vida stepped around Bishop and took in Kasey's diagram. "Oh, no. I think we broke her, Bishop."

Bishop stepped up to the board and took in the detail.

Kasey pointed at her diagram. "This is everything we know so far about the attack on New York City. We know that there is an organization behind the attack. Danilo Lelac told us as much. We ran into the Shinigami when they attacked the Precinct and the language they used here in this very room tells us they are a part of it."

She pointed to the top of the board. "The Master, whoever he is, has something planned for this city. I have seen the attack itself in my visions. Thousands will die, if not hundreds of thousands. The city will be devastated."

She turned to Vida. "I'm not crazy. I can just see the future. If we don't do something about it, the city is going to be destroyed. It might be a day, a week, a month, or a year from now, but at some point, explosions are going to rock this city and our beautiful New York skyline is going to come crumbling down."

Bishop tapped the stick figure on the right-hand side of the white board. "Who is this Langstrode?"

Kasey wrung her hands together. "That, Bishop, is our next victim."

Bishop's eyebrow crept upwards. "What do you mean, our next victim?"

Kasey rocked back and forward on her feet. "I went to visit one of the buildings I'd seen in my vision. 432 Park Avenue. You may have heard about it. It's almost finished."

"Heard about it?" Vida asked. "Everyone's heard of it. Once it's complete, it's going to be the tallest residential building in the city, and one of the tallest in the entire world. What does that have to do with this?"

"It's the only building that goes unscathed in the attack," Kasey answered. "There's something about it. We need to find out what's so special and get ahead of this attack before it happens."

"So, what has Langstrode got to do with the building?" Bishop asked, tapping on the board.

"Langstrode is the developer behind the building," Kasey said. "He is responsible for overseeing the construction. I went to visit the site after the funeral, and he was there. When I confronted him for information about the project, I had a vision."

Vida set his bag down on the examination table and asked, "Just how often do you have these visions?"

"It's hard to predict," Kasey replied. "Sometimes I might go weeks without a vision, but lately they're being becoming more powerful and more frequent."

Bishop turned to Kasey. "Are visions common in your world?"

Kasey shook her head. "No, the gift of prescience is rare, even among witches and wizards. I have never met another who could do it. I've heard stories, but never met anyone who gets them like I do."

"Hmm. But they are becoming more frequent for you?" Bishop asked.

"Absolutely." Kasey nodded. "I was surprised to see one when I came into contact with Langstrode. Most of the visions I've had lately have occurred when I have to touch a dead body."

Bishop looked at the board and then back to Kasey "So, what did you see?".

Kasey licked her lips nervously. "I saw Langstrode get thrown off his building by some thugs."

"Thrown off the building?" Vida gulped loudly.

"That's right. He fell more than ten stories to his death. Fortunately, my vision ended before he hit the pavement."

Bishop put her hand on Kasey's shoulder. "Did you see who did it?"

"There were three of them," Kasey said. "Two of them look like security guards. The kind of private security that wealthy people pay to follow them around and protect them, while they sip expensive wine and eat overpriced food. The third I couldn't see. He was hidden from view by a drop cloth. I heard his voice, but I didn't recognize it. Langstrode tried to buy his way out of whatever trouble he was in, but they weren't having a bit of it. The next thing I knew, the two security guards picked up Langstrode and tossed him off the building."

"If you saw these men again, could you identify them?" Bishop asked.

"I think so," Kasey said. "It happened so fast, but I could try."

"Very well, we'll get a sketch artist working with you on reconstructing their appearance. If we can find them, perhaps we can find out who is behind it."

"While we are at it, we need to look into his family. I got the impression that things are a little turbulent. Seems like any one of them may have wanted him dead. I have to be honest though, after meeting him, I'm more than a little tempted to do nothing and just wait for those goons to throw him off a building. Rid the world of one more toxic snob."

Bishop shook her head as she looked at Kasey. "You know that's not how we do things around here."

Kasey raised both arms defensively. "I'm just kidding. He may have been a jerk, but I don't want to see him dead. No matter how much of a jerk he is, Sal Langstrode and his building are at the heart of everything. Now we just need to find out who wants him dead and stop them before he becomes our next body."

Bishop smiled. "Well, at least we have a head start."

"A head start?" Vida asked.

"Yeah, for once, we know who is going to die before it happens. With that much of a lead, we may just be able to save his life."

Kasey nodded. "I hope so, but we need to narrow down just who might want to kill this guy."

Bishop bent over and collected one of the morgue's battered stools to sit on. Its faux leather seat was scorched.

Kasey grabbed a stool of her own while Vida paced back and forth in front of the white board.

"Look, Langstrode didn't give me a whole lot of time," Kasey started. "From my brief insight into his life, I'd say that anybody who has ever met or spoken to the man might want to kill him."

Bishop raised an eyebrow.

Vida stopped. "He certainly seems like a charmer."

"He couldn't give you any indication as to who might want him dead?" Bishop asked, running her hand through her hair.

Kasey thought about it. "He mentioned things are pretty rocky at home. We should start with his family and work our way out. Then we can move on to investors and others he might have had business dealings with. There are also all the angry tenants that he has had evicted over the years."

"Let's get started," Bishop said tapping her foot impatiently. "The sooner, the better. We can't just idle away our time, or we will have another body on our hands."

Vida shrugged. "Well, without a body, I'm not exactly sure what you expect me to do. This whole new stop the killer before he can do it development is great and all, but it doesn't really play into my particular set of skills."

Kasey laughed, pushing to her feet. "I guess we just have to teach an old dog some new tricks."

"Old dog?" Vida asked, his face scrunched in mock protest. "We are the same age. I may not have killed a werewolf with my bare hands, but there is no way you could mistake this rippling physique for an old man."

Kasey made a show of eying Vida up and down. "It's true, Vida. Your carefully selected diet of beer and pizza has turned you into the formidable killing machine you are today."

Vida patted his stomach self-consciously. "Thanks, Kasey, you are always good for a morning pick me up."

"No need to be a sour grape," Bishop said, standing. "I don't believe for a minute you're a man of so few skills. Let's see if your office escaped unscathed. If your computer is still in one piece, we can run a search on our database to see if we have any records of Langstrode or those he has come in contact with."

Vida wandered over to the door which led to his office. Pushing it open, he let out a loud sigh. "Well, it appears Kasey only barbecued half my office, so we might be in luck with the computer. Bring the chairs. I'm not parting with mine."

Kasey and Bishop scooped up their stools and followed Vida into the office. The first few feet of it were badly charred. The far wall and desk, however, looked like they had only minor staining from the smoke.

Vida flopped down in his office chair and let out a sigh of relief as he reclined the chair.

Reaching down, he pressed his computer's power button, bringing it to life.

As the login screen appeared, Bishop leaned over and stole the keyboard. "Here, let me. I have far better system access.

We'll be able to pull up a lot more information."

Bishop keyed in her password and the desktop appeared, a NYPD crest on a navy-blue background.

"Mind if I drive?" Bishop asked.

Vida slid the mouse over so that it was in front of her. "By all means."

"How does it work?" Kasey asked.

"Well," Bishop began, "our system has records of everyone we've ever booked. It also tracks information on people of interest related to the case."

"People of interest?" Kasey asked, leaning closer.

"Those we have found to have connections with convicted felons, or whom we have suspected of criminal activity but have never succeeded in bringing a case against. We flag them as people of interest just in case. If we find that we keep coming back to them, we dig deeper until we find out what's lurking beneath the surface, then we build a case against them."

"But Langstrode is a developer, not a felon. What are you hoping to find?"

Bishop laughed as she continued typing. "Kasey, this is New York. The two are not mutually exclusive. More than one Upper East side developer has built their fortune on the misery of others. They drive tenants out of old buildings with extortion, blackmail, or bullying. Then they tear down the building and redevelop it. The developing isn't the crime, but often their work practices are on the fringe. We're checking the system to see if Langstrode or any of his associates are on the wrong side of the line. It's possible the vision you saw was a falling out between Langstrode and some of his business partners."

"I see," Kasey answered. "What have we got? Anything interesting?"

"Just a minute," Bishop answered, beating away on the keyboard. "These machines really aren't that quick."

There was a blip on the screen as a large list appeared.

"I may have spoken too soon," Bishop said.

Vida shrugged. "I may or may not have upgraded the hardware. The old one was unbearably slow."

"Nerd," Bishop chided.

"Proud of it," Vida replied with a grin.

Kasey studied the screen as the search results populated. A handful of results appeared before the cursor changed, signaling the search had been completed.

Bishop sighed. "To be honest, it's a lot less than I was expecting. Langstrode doesn't appear to be affiliated with any known criminal organizations. We have a few complaints here from ex-tenants, but as I said, those are to be expected. No one likes being kicked out of their home."

Kasey scanned through the results. The second to last drew her attention. "What about this one?" She pointed at the screen. "It says Langstrode received a series of death threats when they tore down a set of apartments in 2015.Those apartments are where his new skyscraper is being built. That's 432 Park Avenue."

"You're right," Bishop replied. Clicking on the result, she opened the report. "According to the file, the death threats were tracked to one of the tenants who had been evicted. A man by the name of Vincent Anders."

"Where is Mr. Anders now?" Vida asked.

Bishop's fingers danced over the keyboard. "Let's find out."

When the result appeared, Bishop opened it.

"Well that's a dead end," Vida said.

"What do you mean?" Bishop asked.

"That number down there," Vida answered, pointing at the screen. "Whoever made the note hasn't labeled it clearly, but there's a reason the investigation was closed."

Kasey counted out the digits and realized what Vida was getting at. "It's the identification number for the office of the Chief medical examiner. Every morgue in the city has one. It means Mr. Anders is dead. The OCME processed the body themselves, probably due to the investigation that followed the death threats. They will have wanted to make sure it wasn't murder."

"Like I said, a dead end," Vida said.

Kasey reached over and gave Vida a shove. "I got it the first time, but that was by far your worst pun yet. I was letting it slide."

"Give it time, Kasey," he said with a grin. "I will grow on you. Like a fine wine, I get better with age."

"Only in your dreams. In any event, you're right. If Anders died last year, he can't be our man."

Bishop nodded. "So, Sal is clean. Relatively speaking, no past issues with the department and no known entanglements with any criminal organizations."

Kasey drummed her fingers on the desk. "Try his family. From his comments earlier, his situation at home is less than ideal."

"Family, huh," Bishop mused. "You think it might be the wife? Having hubby thrown off a building seems extreme. A divorce would be less messy."

"But so much more expensive," Vida chimed in. "A divorcee gets half the estate, but a widow gets it all."

"That's cold," Vida said.

"But true," Kasey answered. "Anyway, isn't it always the spouse? That's what you told me."

"More often than not," Bishop replied. "But as far as I can see, Cynthia is as clean as a whistle. No ties to any criminal organization. Hasn't even had a speeding ticket or parking fine in the last twelve months. If she is planning something, we're not going to find it in here. We'll have to keep eyes on her."

"What about kids?" Kasey asked.

"According to this, Sal and Cynthia have two kids. Martin is twenty-six and Alicia who is twenty-one." Bishop kept searching. "Alicia is studying, but it looks like Martin has been busy. Two DUIs in his late teens, and a few months ago he was picked up on a drug charge. Methamphetamines. Based on the quantity, he should have been charged with intention to distribute, but it looks like he was only charged with possession. Judge let him off with community service for a first-time offense."

Kasey shook her head. "Privilege of being in the one percent, I guess."

"Perhaps," Bishop said, "but the drugs were still seized. That's going to leave Martin with a problem. With the way these dealers operate, he'll owe his boss a sizable wad of cash. Probably can't ask daddy for money to fend off his Drug Boss."

"Think that's enough to get Langstrode killed?" Kasey asked.

"People have been killed for a lot less. We'll keep digging but for the time being we'll keep eyes on Sal and his family. See if we can't work out who has it in for him."

"Where do you want to start?" Kasey asked.

"Martin," Bishop said, standing up and straightening her jacket. "He just has so many friends I think we should meet."

CHAPTER 4

Kasey and Bishop had tailed Martin from his home to Amsterdam Avenue, where he had disappeared into a pawn shop almost two hours ago. The pawn shop had a narrow frontage dominated by several floor-to-ceiling windows. The displays consisted of second hand jewelry and the store's garish red and yellow signage, offering payday loans in addition to its second-hand goods.

The store was one of several occupying the first floor of an aging apartment building. The sign hanging in the front window announced the store to be shut. A little suspicious given it was barely midday.

Kasey loathed being stuck in the car. Waiting had never been her strongpoint, and stakeouts were becoming one of her least favorite activities in her assignment at the NYPD. Fortunately, Bishop had come through on the lunch front.

Food makes everything better.

Kasey sank her teeth into the burrito. She let out a muffled moan as the chili seasoning set her tongue alight. The burrito had clearly been made fresh to order, not the pre-packaged garbage that had become all too common in takeaway stores. Jesús clearly knew his way around the kitchen.

"I've gotta say, the stake-out food is better than I'd expected," Kasey said, licking the spice from her lips.

"It's an art form," Bishop replied. "You spend enough time on stake-outs here in the city, and you'll learn which restaurants and food trucks are worth eating at, and which you should avoid like the plague. I found Jesús a couple of years back. He was a lifesaver."

"Oh yeah?" Kasey answered. "How so?"

Bishop unwrapped her burrito. "We were staking out a man who had killed his wife. She'd been found dead, supposedly a victim of a home invasion. The case stank but we didn't have enough evidence to charge him. So, we surveilled the place for days. Eventually, a mistress showed up. We got a search warrant for her apartment and found the murder weapon, along with several bloodstained items of the wife's clothing. She went down for murder and he went down as an accessory. Unfortunately, the stake-out lasted the better part of three days. Jesús kept us from going hungry."

Kasey tapped the dashboard. "You were stuck in the car for three days?"

Bishop laughed. "Sometimes the car isn't discreet enough. So, for comfort or discretion, particularly on the longer stakeouts, we try to rent an empty apartment with a view of the target."

"What makes you think this pawn shop is special?" Kasey asked, peeling down the wrapper on her burrito.

"Well, that particular establishment is owned and operated by one Lester Colton. He's one of the city's less upstanding citizens. By all accounts, he's a loan shark, but Martin's presence here might indicate he's diversified his operations to include narcotics. The store is a convenient front."

"Front?" Kasey asked, taking another bite of her burrito.

"For laundering money," Bishop explained. "Selling drugs produces a lot of cash, but that cash can't be used as freely as they might like, without it being picked up by the IRS or DEA.

"If Lester is dealing, then the store is a convenient place to clean his money. He takes the dirty cash and loans it to people in the form of payday loans. Then when they repay it, along with an exorbitant interest rate, Lester gets clean cash and a tidy profit."

Kasey nodded appreciatively. "Seems clever."

"Oh, it would be. The only problem with their business model is their dealers. Drug dealers inevitably get caught. They are far sloppier than men like Lester. Boys like Martin get caught up trying to make a quick buck. Then the District Attorney gets them to flip on their boss in exchange for a plea deal. Takes time but eventually the department scoops up someone not willing to do the jail time and the carefully constructed criminal enterprise comes crashing down."

"So, we shut him down?" Kasey asked.

Bishop shook her head. "I wish it was that easy, Kasey. Drug cases take considerably more time than homicide to build and prosecute. Dealers have the cash to pay for the best representation. The department won't drag one to court unless the case is airtight.

"Lester is safe for the time being. We'll bounce the lead to narcotics and they will start working the case. In the meantime, we'll see what Martin's up to. If Lester is involved, it adds credence to our theory that Martin may be short of cash. Langstrode's murder might be connected to his son's money problems."

Kasey swallowed and cleared her throat. "I guess we just need to work out whether Lester is owed the money or if he's lending it."

"Precisely," Bishop answered. "If he's lending it, he's just one more loan shark profiting off another's poor decisions. Not great, but not inherently illegal. If it's Lester's drugs that Martin had seized, then there is a chance he may take it out on Sal, as you saw in your vision."

There was movement at the storefront as the glass door swung inward.

Kasey perked up. "Bishop."

"I see it," Bishop answered.

Martin had been thrown into the street. He hit the sidewalk and rolled onto his back. A surly man in a tight black shirt tossed a backpack at Martin, before stepping back into the store. The door swung shut.

Martin struggled to his feet. His sandy hair was tussled, and a large bruise was forming on his right cheek. He dusted himself off and tucked his shirt back into his slacks. Picking up his backpack, he slung it over his shoulder and set off down the street.

"I think it's time to have a chat with our friend," Bishop said, setting her burrito on the dashboard.

"Here?" Kasey asked.

"No, we'll pick him up down the street. It may be an unmarked car, but the last thing we want is for Lester to know we were sniffing around."

Bishop turned the key in the ignition and the engine rumbled to life. Signaling with her blinker, she pulled out into traffic and then rolled down the street after Martin.

Ahead of Martin, the crosswalk turned red. Glancing at the light, he turned left and strode down the street. Reaching the next intersection, he stepped out onto the crosswalk as Bishop pulled into it. Easing to a stop just in front of him.

"Hey! Watch where you're going!" Martin shouted at the car.

Bishop lowered her window and flashed her badge. "Martin Langstrode. Detective Bishop, 9th Precinct. We'd like to have a chat."

Martin glanced up and down the street.

"Don't even think about it, Martin. Do you really think you can outrun us, after the beating you just took? You're barely staying on your feet."

"I'm fine," Martin replied, his lip quivering as he spoke.

"I'm sure you are, Martin," Bishop said. "Why don't you get in the car and tell us how fine you are. Don't worry, Lester's thugs aren't watching us here."

"What do you know about Lester?" Martin asked, halting.

"Enough," Bishop answered. "Now get in the car and talk to us quietly. Otherwise, we'll be forced to drag you down to the station very publicly. You wouldn't want Lester hearing you were down at a police station five minutes after he gave you that black eye, would you?"

"Lester knows I'm not a snitch," Martin protested.

"Does he, Martin? I don't know about that. I certainly wouldn't stake my life on his trusting disposition. Now get in the car."

Martin scanned the street again and then reached for the door handle. He took one last look up the street before opening the door.

After clambering into the back seat of the car, Martin shut the door and fastened his seat belt. "Right, now what is it you want?"

"Let's find somewhere a little more discreet than the middle of the street," Bishop answered as she rolled down the road.

Kasey waited quietly, studying Martin in the rearview mirror as Bishop guided the car into a quiet side street.

"What are you looking at?" Martin asked.

"Huh?" Kasey answered.

"You're staring. What are you looking at?" Martin asked as he slid his hair back behind his ears.

"After meeting your father, you're not quite what I was expecting, that's all," Kasey said.

"Hmph. So my father sent you. Great, what does the old man want now?" Martin muttered.

Bishop pulled over, then turned to face Martin. "First, your father didn't send us. We're following a lead. Second, I'm asking the questions, got it?"

Martin shrugged. "Sure. What do you want to know?"

"How about we start with why you look like you've gone a round with Mike Tyson. Did you walk into a door repeatedly or is that a souvenir from Lester?" Kasey asked.

Martin stared straight back at Bishop. "I think you already know the answer to that one."

"I guess we do," Bishop mused. "How about we move on to the why, then. Tell me, Marty, why did Lester try to rearrange your face? What did you do to disappoint him?"

"You know what he does, right? I owe him money. This is my reminder that I'm late."

"I would have thought you have easier means of getting finance than someone like Lester?" Bishop prodded.

"Oh, you mean my family?" Martin scoffed. "Yeah, right. I may still live at home, but they've cut me off. Second time Dad had to weigh in on a DUI, he stopped paying my allowance."

"So, you took up dealing to bolster your bank account?" Bishop asked.

"No. Not at first. Turns out, flipping burgers just doesn't go as far as I am used to. I needed some extra cash and there's plenty of it around. I just needed something people wanted. That's where the drugs came in, but you guys know all about that. It's a matter of record now"

"Who are you slinging for? Is it Lester?" Bishop asked looking over her shoulder.

Martin looked down at his feet. "I'm not answering that one, detective. Your boys threw the book at me when I was at the station for possession. I'm not saying a word."

He folded his arms over his chest.

"Even after Lester cleaned the concrete with your face?" Kasey asked.

"This," he said, pointing to his face, "will look positively affectionate compared to what will happen if I answer that question. Talking about my crimes is one thing but snitching on others is another. They'll kill me, and I rather like living, so thanks, but no thanks."

Bishop tried a different tact. "Any idea who would want to kill your father?"

"What?" Martin leaned forward. "No idea, why?"

"We've received word of a credible threat against him from one of our informants. We were wondering if your friendship with Lester Colton has anything to do with it."

Martin was silent as he leaned back in the seat.

"Martin?" Bishop probed tapping her hands on the steering wheel.

"I doubt it, detective. Lester might rough up people who break their payment plans but killing is bad for business. Dead men don't pay their debts."

"But it's not your father's debt, is it, Martin?" Bishop countered. "If Daddy dies and you inherit a share of his considerable estate, that would leave you in a position to pay off your debt and live comfortably for the rest of your life. Maybe not as comfortably as he has, but you'd be a long way from flipping burgers. What do you think, Kasey?"

Kasey nodded. "Sounds like motive to me. Maybe Marty is in on the plan, maybe not. Either way, he stands to gain from his father's death. That's motive, for sure."

"I'm right here," Martin said, "and that is insane. You think I'd kill my father to pay off my debts. That's just crazy. He may have cut me off, but he also kept me out of jail. You are way off base there."

"Convince me, Marty," Bishop said cocking her head. "From where I'm sitting, you seem to have the most to gain from your father's death.

"Do your research, detective. After the drug charge, Dad cut me out of the will. So, if he dies, I get nothing. If anything, I need him to stay alive as long as possible."

"Why is that?" Kasey asked.

"Mom and I don't get along. When I was caught with the drugs, Mom wanted to toss me out of the house, but Dad wouldn't allow it. If Dad dies, mom and my sister will get everything, and she'll almost certainly kick me out. Detective, you should be looking into her. If you think it's one of us that's going to kill him, she has a hell of a lot more to gain than I do."

"Why would she kill her husband?" Kasey asked. From Sal's earlier comments, she had her suspicions, but she wanted to hear what Martin would say about his parents.

"Husband." Martin scoffed. "That word doesn't really describe their relationship anymore. Husband and wife, nah, more like two people coexisting under one roof. She's been cheating on him for years and he knows it. If he'd had the foresight to get a pre-nup, I'm sure they would already be divorced."

"So, who is the lucky man?" Bishop asked.

"Right now?" Martin asked. "I believe it's her yoga instructor, Leith. He spends far too much time at the house. I doubt what they're doing qualifies as yoga, but it might give you two some insight into who might want my Dad dead. If it's not Mom, it might well be Leith wanting to move in permanently."

"Not a fan?" Kasey asked.

"Of what, yoga?" Martin asked. "Couldn't care less, but the guy is a fraud. I've seen more convincing yoga in Central Park. Leith needs to Nama-stay out of our house."

"I see. Well we'll look into Leith and see what we find. In the meantime, keep your nose clean, Martin. We'll be in touch if we have any more questions."

"I don't suppose I could get a lift back to the Upper East Side," Martin asked.

Kasey raised an eyebrow at Bishop.

Bishop shook her head. "Sorry, Marty, we're the police, not an Uber. You got yourself cut-off and topped it off with the DUI's. I don't think we'd be doing you any favors if we spared you the consequences of your actions."

"Thanks." Martin rolled his eyes.

"Out you hop," Bishop said, motioning with her fingers. "The fresh air and exercise will do you good."

"Uh-huh," Martin answered, opening the door and getting out of the car. He yanked his backpack off the backseat, then slammed the door.

Bishop put on her seatbelt and Kasey followed suit.

As Bishop pulled out into traffic, Kasey looked at her and asked, "What are you thinking? Do you believe him?"

Bishop cocked her head. "It's possible. His story is easy enough to check out. All we need is a copy of the will. If he's not in it, his motive disappears. It's always possible Lester or one of his associates could be involved but from what Marty was saying, this Leith might be worth taking a run at. Mrs. Langstrode, too."

"Are we seeing them now?" Kasey asked.

"Soon. I've got to swing by the station and take care of a few things first. We'll head over there this afternoon and see what she has to say for herself."

Kasey nodded.

I only hope that is soon enough.

Her biggest worry was that her vision had not given her any indication of when Sal would be killed. The building was still under construction in her vision which meant that Sal would be killed before it was complete.

With its grand opening set for December, they might have as much as a few months or as little as a few hours to solve the case. There was no way of knowing.

The nagging feeling in her stomach told her time was running out.

CHAPTER 5

Kasey was crouching as she rummaged through the cupboard in search of a much-needed pick-me-up. The station's kitchen was bare, and the coffee pot was empty. Kasey's stomach growled. Dinner was still hours away and she was starving.

Spotting a box of coffee sachets at the back of the shelf, she let out a whoop. Grabbing it, she backed out of the cupboard. Standing up, she shook the box.

Nothing.

"Who does that?" Kasey muttered to herself, throwing the empty box on the counter.

"Something wrong, Ms. Chase?" a familiar voice called from the kitchen's door.

"Yeah, some jackass drank all the coffee and then put the empty box back in the cupboard." She replied without thinking.

Silence greeted Kasey's angry outburst. When there was no response her stomach sank.

I know that voice.

Kasey spun to see who had interrupted her. Chief West was leaning against the door jamb, his arms folded and his glasses resting halfway down his nose.

"Chief!" Kasey yelped. "I'm so sorry. I didn't realize it was you..."

The chief's mouth slowly creased upward into a smile. "Relax, Kasey, I can get a little hangry myself from time to time."

Kasey leaned back against the counter. "What can I do for you, chief? I must say, I'm struggling to believe you would eat anything from the station's kitchen."

The chief chuckled. "Oh, I used to, Kasey, make no mistake, but the fourth floor does come with its perks and it's been a while since I've needed to wander down here."

"What brings you here now?" she asked.

"You, Ms. Chase." He stepped into the kitchen. "There were a few things I wanted to talk to you about. I saw you enter the kitchen and thought now was as good a time as any."

"Should I sit down?" Kasey asked, pointing to the table.

"I think I might," the chief volunteered. "It's been a long day and these old legs don't cope like they used to." He strode over to the table and pulled out a chair, then flopped into it. "Please, grab a seat."

Kasey pulled out the chair and spun it around so that she was able to lean on the chair rest as she faced the Chief.

The chief smiled. "You're not like most people around here, Ms. Chase."

"Is that a good thing or a bad thing, chief?" Kasey asked.

He pondered the question. "I haven't decided yet. Your time here has come amid trying times. These few weeks have been some of the most devastating this precinct has ever faced."

Kasey's heart sank. The Shinigami assault on the precinct had cost the lives of many officers. While Kasey hadn't known it at the time, she had inadvertently drawn their ire as she had tried to solve the murder of Cyrus Pillar. That knowledge was a heavy burden to bear.

The chief continued. "That said, in the last few weeks, we've caught a serial killer and brought Wendell Samson and his crew to justice. You were instrumental in both cases. When the OCME recommended you for a secondment here, I was skeptical, but you've acquitted yourself well."

"Chief, I don't understand..."

He held up his hand. "Patience, Ms. Chase. I'm getting to my point. The OCME has asked for you back. They want to end your secondment, and have you return to your former duties as soon as possible.

Her heart skipped a beat. She leaned forward in her chair. "What do you mean?"

"It means, Kasey, your secondment here at the NYPD has been terminated. With the OCME requesting your return to your former duties, there is little we can do."

"But," Kasey protested, "I'm busy here. We have cases. I can't just drop everything and return to my old job." She drew a deep breath as she struggled for words.

Returning to the OCME should have made her happy. It was the job she had always wanted, but the timing couldn't have been worse.

With the attack on New York City drawing nearer, she was determined to devote her efforts to defending the city. That would be difficult to do if she was stuck in the basement morgue of the Chief Medical Examiner's Office.

"What's wrong, Kasey?" the Chief asked. "I thought the job at the OCME would have been good news. When you came here, you seemed entirely put out by the whole transfer. If I might make an observation, you now appear entirely unhappy at the thought of having to return. Why is that? What has changed?"

Kasey pondered on the question. Something had certainly changed. She could feel it. There was something different about working cases with Bishop. Being on the front lines and saving people's lives had proved far more exciting than simply performing autopsies after the fact. While her work at the OCME had been important, her time at the NYPD had been transformative.

Kasey wrung her fingers as she looked into the chief's steely eyes. "Chief, I know you were concerned when I arrived, and I don't blame you. The circumstances of my transfer would have had most people up in arms. Assaulting a colleague should have gotten me sacked but instead, I ended up here. I have to be honest, as hectic as it has been, I've really developed a taste for it."

The Chief leaned forward, resting his hand on one knee as he spoke. "What are you saying, Kasey? Are you saying you don't want to go back?"

She sat up straight. "Is that an option?"

"It could be," he said. "You know the OCME is understaffed. Keeping your position vacant the last few weeks hasn't been easy for her. It wouldn't be fair to expect her to keep it for you indefinitely."

"What are you saying, chief?"

"What I'm saying, Kasey, is that you can have one job or the other, but you can't have both. If you want to work here at the Ninth Precinct and continue working cases with Bishop, then it can happen. With your case closing rate, I'm more than happy to go to bat for you, but it will require you to leave the OCME and take up a full-time post with the NYPD. You won't be able to simply go back when you feel like it. It would be permanent."

She let out a long low breath. "How long do I have to make the decision?"

"Five pm," he said. "I need to give them an answer before I leave today. Which means I need to hear from you by then. Have a think about it and let me know where you land. It goes without saying but I'm going to say it, anyway. We would be pleased to keep you, if you'll stay."

Kasey smiled. The chief's endorsement was high praise.

"Thanks, chief. It really means a lot to me. I wasn't expecting this. Please let me have a think about, and I'll get back to you today."

The chief stood up, adjusted his belt, and tucked in his shirt that had begun to break free. "One other thing, Kasey. You said you were working a lead. With the gala shooting closed, I wasn't aware of any open homicide cases. What are you working on?"

Kasey realized too late that she had opened a can of worms. The Langstrode case wasn't technically even on the board at the precinct. Doing so would require some sort of evidence or basis for the threat against Langstrode's life. Evidence she wasn't in a position to provide. Not yet, at least. The NYPD didn't tend to work cases based on visions.

"Well, it isn't quite there yet. At least not a homicide. We received a tip that a high-profile businessman might be in danger. Bishop and I are running down the lead. We are hoping we might be able to head this one off at the pass. Save his life and save it from ever becoming a case."

The chief nodded appreciatively. "And the informant is credible?"

"She's proved credible in the past," Kasey answered, referring to herself in the third person.

"And the target, anyone we know?" the chief asked.

"He is a developer on the upper east side," Kasey answered. "A man by the name of Sal Langstrode."

"Sal Langstrode?" The chief gasped. "I know him. He's worth a small fortune. You have your work cut out for you, though. More than a few people would like to see him floating face down in the bay."

"What makes you say that? We've looked into his files. Doesn't seem we have a whole lot of information on him."

"No, that's not the kind of information we keep on record," the chief answered. "They are just rumors, really. No one has ever been able to prove anything."

Kasey sat up. "Prove anything about what?"

The chief paused, as if considering how to answer the question. "Well, let's just say that Sal is a ruthless businessman. He's developed several buildings with other developers and investors and always managed to come out on top. Several of them of wound up in jail. One of them disappeared from the face of the Earth, never to be seen again. And another was cut out of the profit due to some legal wrangling on Langstrode's part. If I were in that line of work,

I'd think twice before developing at all. I'd certainly think twice before going into business with him, that's for sure."

Kasey shook her head. "We had no idea about any of that."

"As I said, there was never anything that could stick. Langstrode is as slippery as they get. Most of that is just rumor and conjecture I have heard at functions I've attended. You know what they say though?"

"I do," Kasey answered. "Where there's smoke there's fire."

The chief smiled. "You're learning quick. Now, you just need to find out where the fire is. If someone is gunning for Langstrode, you can be sure that they have past or present dealings with him. Either of those considerations should help narrow your target suspects."

Kasey nodded. "Thanks, chief. I'll let Bishop know.

The Chief turned and made for the door. Looking over his shoulder, he called, "Remember, Kasey, five pm."

"Yes, chief," Kasey answered, standing.

Left alone to her thoughts, Kasey considered what chief had said. The OCME or the NYPD. It was a lot to consider.

She thought of her old boss. Julie Sampson had gone out on a limb for her. If it wasn't for her interference, Kasey would have been out of work entirely, run over by the political and fiscal influence of the Ainsleys.

Kasey owed Sampson a lot. Both her career, and her reputation had been protected by the chief medical examiner. The transfer to the NYPD would be leaving her old boss in the lurch and the thought of that didn't sit well with Kasey at all. On the other hand, she loved working at the NYPD.

Had life been normal, she might have returned to the OCME out of loyalty to Sampson.

But there were other considerations.

Her visions had been clear and consistent. Each day it drew nearer. While the Shinigami had suffered a setback, somewhere out there, their master plotted the destruction of the city and the misery of millions of people. That wasn't a threat Kasey could ignore, the attack on New York was coming.

In her heart, she knew it was up to her to make a difference. Her vision was the only warning New York had that such a threat even existed. She considered how she might feel if she disregarded the threat and lives were lost as a result of her inaction.

Sure, she could try to pursue leads from the OCME, but the medical examiner's office had far less resources than the NYPD. Not to mention her ability to carry on her investigation or interrogate suspects would be reduced or disappear entirely.

The difficult choice was one she wasn't keen to make. Pushing it from her mind, she made her way down to the morgue.

Entering the battered room, she found Vida standing with Bishop at the white board.

Vida turned to her." Speak of the devil and she appears. Were your ears burning?"

"No. Why?" Kasey asked. "What's going on?"

Vida's mouth peaked upward into a grin. "I was just telling Bishop, here, what a miracle it was that the pair of you left the station to run down a lead and didn't come back with a dead body. I've gotten so used to the chaos that follows you around, that I half expected you to bring a friend back with you, and when I say friend, I mean a cadaver."

"Ha-ha. Very funny, Vida. Besides, it's still early. At this rate, you might well end up on the table."

"You can't do that, Kasey. Without me, you would have to do all the work yourself, and we both know, even you can't keep up with that pace.

Kasey smiled. "You're right, Vida. I guess I have to keep you around for now. If you keep bandying about my powers, though, it won't be me that comes looking for you."

Vida paused, biting off his retort.

Clearly, he remembered the visit the ADI had paid Kasey earlier and he was not keen to see them again.

Taking advantage of the silence, Bishop said, "So, where are we on the case?".

Kasey approached the white board and picked up the marker. "Well, we struck out with Martin, he certainly has his issues, but he seems to have no motive. He needs his father alive, so I doubt he's our man."

"But he was awfully quick to point the finger at his mother. We need to take a closer look at her." Bishop gestured at the board. "Martin seemed to think his mother is being unfaithful. That could be a motive. If Langstrode dies, she ends up with everything. Far more profitable than a divorce."

"You have a point." Kasey scribbled Cynthia's name on the board. "It could easily be her, or whoever she is fooling around with. Martin seemed to think that the yoga teacher might be spending a little more time doing the downward dog than is necessary."

Bishop nodded. "It's time to pay Mrs. Langstrode a visit. If she knows we are looking around, there is a chance she will slip up and make a mistake, give us something we can use to nail her."

"If it's her," Kasey said. "If it's not, Langstrode is in just as much danger as before, and we'll have been focusing on the wrong suspect the whole time."

Bishop tapped the board. "You think there is a more likely candidate?"

"I don't know," Kasey replied. "The murder certainly looked well-orchestrated. I don't know that Mrs. Langstrode or her yoga teacher move in the right circles to have that kind of access."

"What are you getting at?" Vida asked.

"I know we wrote off his business dealings earlier," Kasey began, "but on my way down here, I ran into the chief. He asked what we are working on and I told him about the case. He seemed to think Langstrode's past business dealings have been sketchy.

"No charges have ever been filed, but West seems to think that more than one of Langstrode's previous partners have been stung by him. He has a reputation for taking advantage of his partners and coming out on top. Perhaps we need to take another look at who he has worked with previously. One of them might be our man."

"Or woman," Vida suggested.

Kasey had to concede the point. "I suppose you're right. Man or woman, we don't know. But there is every chance his murder might have something to do with his partners, past or present. Vida, look into anyone he has or is working with. After all, 432 Park Avenue is a monstrous project. He can't be the only party involved."

Vida rubbed his hands together. "Well, since we have a quiet morning on our hands here, I'll dig into Langstrode's business dealings. You two should check out his wife, find out if we have an axe murderer on our hands."

Kasey chuckled at the reference.

"I'll grab my coat." She made her way over to the bench and snatched it. As she did, the phone in the pocket began to ring. She pulled out the phone and checked the caller ID. Private number. She answered the call and held it up to her ear. "Hello, who is this?"

"Ah, Miss Chase." The voice sounded familiar, but Kasey couldn't quite place where she had heard before. "It's agent Clark from the ADI. We met the other week at your work."

Kasey's mind raced. The Anti Discovery Initiative, or ADI, were the arm of the Arcane Council's law enforcement branch. They were tasked with safeguarding the secrecy of the magical community and enforcing the Arcane Council's laws. Clark was one of the agents that had been dispatched to warn Kasey after she had used her magic on Brad Tesco.

The agent had been clear: Further incident would result in dire repercussions. Had they somehow witnessed her using her magic against the Shinigami? Did they know Vida and Bishop had learned her secret?

Clark's voice carrying through the phone was not a welcome surprise.

She swallowed hard. "What can I do for you, Agent Clark?"

"Miss Chase, I need you to come into the ADI at once."

She paced, chewing her nail. "I'm at work, Clark. I can't just blow it off whenever you need me too. I have things to do here."

I'm sure you do, Miss Chase, but it's not a request— it's a requirement. 85 Chambers Street. Come now," Clarke said.

Before she could reply, he hung up.

CHAPTER 6

K asey emerged from the subway station and found herself standing on Broadway. Opposite her lay City Hall with its sprawling park and fountain. According to her phone GPS, the address Clark had given her was just around the corner.

Heading up Broadway, Kasey passed a retail storefront. The entire first floor of the building was occupied by a bank. The external facade of the building was a simple yet striking combination of black stonework and large glass pane windows.

The street beside her was packed, and Kasey didn't envy the commuters. This end of Manhattan could be a nightmare at any point in the day. It was the reason Kasey had decided to take the subway in the first place.

She rounded the corner, heading for number 85. She was so intent on her destination that she missed the figure leaning against the wall of the bank.

"Miss Chase, it's good to see you again."

The sudden motion to her left caused her to leap a mile. Her heart raced.

Turning, she spotted the source of the voice: a stocky man in an ill-fitting suit. The trousers looked like they were for someone 6 inches taller, and the coat was clearly straining to contain the man's broad shoulders. The man was a good deal shorter than Kasey, but what he lacked in height he more than made up for in breadth.

Kasey recognized him from his earlier visit to the Ninth Precinct.

"Clark, after our last little chat, I can't say I was excited to hear from you, much less to be dragged out of work and across town. What's going on?"

Clark swept his hand toward the bank. "If you would follow me, you will have your answers soon enough."

Kasey dug in her heels and raised an eyebrow. "Unless I get an answer now, I'm not going anywhere."

Clark raised his hands in an effort to calm her down. "Take it easy, Kasey. This isn't at all related to our previous encounter. The Council is pleased to see you took your warning seriously. By all accounts, you have been on your best behavior."

Kasey rested her hands on her hips. From Clark's reaction, it seemed the Council had no idea that her secret had leaked out. When the Shinigami had attacked the Ninth Precinct, Bishop and Vida had witnessed magic in action—from both the Shinigami, and from Kasey.

It was a course of events the Arcane Council would be furious about, should they become aware of it. When Clark had summonsed her, Kasey had feared the worst. Now it appeared the Council was after something else and Kasey wasn't sure whether she should be relieved or concerned. Certainly, she didn't want the Council to discover what Vida and Bishop knew. Their reaction would be heavy-handed and potentially dangerous to her friends.

One thought niggled at the back of her mind.

If discovery wasn't the Council's agenda, why had she been summonsed?

The last thing she wanted was to become entangled with the Council while she was devoting all of her effort to thwarting the attack on New York.

"So, are you going to tell me why we are here?" Kasey asked.

Clark scanned the street. "We're in the middle of the city. This isn't the time or the place. Come with me, and I will tell you everything. Stay here, and I cannot say a word. The whole purpose of our organization is to keep our world hidden and safe. I'm not going to discuss its most confidential agenda in the middle of a crowded city street." He looked her up and down. "Are you coming or not?"

Kasey tapped her foot. "So, I have a choice in that?"

Clark's left hand rested on his belt. "You always have a choice. The Council isn't going to make you do anything, not while you abide by its rules. They would, however, like to speak with you and they would like to speak with you now. Suffice it to say, while you may refuse, it will influence your future relationship with them and that would be less than ideal for you, given your track record."

Kasey balled her fist reflexively. "Is that a threat?"

Clark raised his hand into a stopping motion. "No, it's simply a reminder that you've crossed paths with them once already. You are young, and you are living here in New York City, the very heart of their jurisdiction. Wisdom dictates that you would at least give them the time of day."

"Very well," Kasey conceded. "Where are we going?"

"Council headquarters, of course." Clark pointed to the bank. "Follow me, please."

"You want me to believe that the Arcane Council's headquarters are located in a bank on Broadway?"

Clarke's mouth fell open. "You've never been to the Council Chambers?"

"Nope."

Clark smiled. "Then you're in for a treat. To answer your question, it's not in the bank. It's under the bank, and not just the bank—it stretches several blocks in every direction. The bank is simply the easiest entry for a member of the ADI. There are other entrances located through Lower Manhattan. A single entrance would be too obvious. The Council finds it beneficial to have a multitude of entrances scattered across several city blocks. That way, we don't draw any unnecessary attention. As for the ADI, agents in suits coming and going from a bank is hardly newsworthy. It's an extremely convenient cover."

Kasey followed Clark as he rounded the corner onto Broadway. As he approached the bank, its large glass doors opened to greet him. He walked straight past the bank of ATMs and continued across the lobby.

The left-hand side of the room was lined with a counter, manned by an army of bank tellers. Customers waited in lines for the next available teller.

Clark paid them no heed as he traversed the lobby. Reaching a door with a security panel beside it, he produced his identification. It was the same badge he'd flashed Kasey weeks before when they had first met. As the surface of the ID passed over the scanner, there was a click. Clark pushed open the door.

A narrow hall led to a small atrium and a series of elevators. Clark pressed the call button and waited patiently, tapping his ID against his other hand as the elevator descended.

When the doors parted, he stepped into the elevator and Kasey followed. He mashed the button to close the elevator's doors. As soon as they were shut, he fanned open the ID again and waved it across the panel of buttons.

As the ID passed over the buttons, another row appeared. Kasey's eyes went wide. Unlike the buttons for the floors above, which were green, the new buttons were black with gold trim. They read simply B1, B2, B3 and so on. There was more than a dozen of them.

Clark pressed the button labeled B15 and turned to Kasey. "The Council's Chambers are located on the 15th level. Only a sitting Council Member, a member of the ADI, or someone with preapproved clearance can reach that level. Even should a normal manage to make it back here, they only have access to the floors above."

"What is above us?" Kasey asked.

"Administrative departments dealing with many of the different facets of our world. They handle the interaction of the Council with the world around us. It's a full-time job. At least 200 staff man those offices, not to mention the bank employees out there."

The elevator began to descend.

"You mean all of those tellers are witches and wizards?" Kasey asked.

"Every one of them," Clark replied. "Even witches and wizards need jobs, you know that. Money doesn't grow on trees and not everything we need can simply be conjured up with a thought. Isn't that why you work at the precinct?"

Kasey laughed. "I work there because I wanted to get away from the World of Magic. I never wanted to be a part of this world."

"Why is that?" Clark asked. "If you don't mind me asking."

"Magic made my childhood a misery. Normal kids might be a tease but you give those children magic and they become truly cruel. I didn't want anything to do with it."

"Well, life has a way of pulling you back in," he said. "Speaking of, the Council is wanting to debrief you. I understand you met with the chairman, Mr. Ainsley, but the remainder of the Council would like to be briefed both on your encounter with the killer, Danilo Lelac, and your experience at the Gala Shooting. As you know, the head of the ADI was killed that night."

Kasey looked down at the floor of the elevator. The memory of the massacre at the gala still unsettled her. Looking up, she brushed her hair back out of her face and answered. "I know. I was there. I tried to help him, but he was already dead."

"Cyrus was a good man, and a great leader," Clark replied. "We'll miss him here."

The elevator came to a halt and its doors opened.

"Follow me, Miss Chase."

Stepping out of the elevator, Kasey found herself in an expansive atrium. The polished porcelain tiles seemed to gleam beneath her feet. She could almost see her reflection in them. Artwork hung on wood panel walls. What little furniture there was, looked like it had been sourced from one of Manhattan's many antique stores. Each piece of finely turned wood would have had to have been crafted carefully by hand for hours to produce the chairs she now strode past.

Or maybe they cheated with a little magic.

At the other end of the chamber, a series of metal detectors lined the walls. On either side of the detectors stood a man in a suit.

More ADI.

Clark made for the metal detectors and strolled straight through them. The machine beeped wildly but Clark simply flashed his badge and was waved through by his colleagues. Kasey stepped through the detectors and they went off. Both men in suits stepped toward her.

Kasey raised her hands. "Easy, boys, it's okay. I'm with the NYPD. I have a permit to carry this weapon."

She tilted her head toward the gun on her belt.

The ADI agent on her right held out his hand. "Be that as it may, you aren't permitted to carry it here. Hand it over and it will be returned to you when you leave."

Kasey unholstered her Glock and passed it to the agent.

The agent pointed to the metal detectors. "Ma'am, would you mind stepping through the machines again?"

Kasey sighed and took several steps backward, passing through the frame. Nothing happened. She then stepped back through the detector once more.

Satisfied that nothing was out of the ordinary, the agent waved her through. "You're free to go. Please stay with your escort at all times."

Agent Clark barely glanced at her as he approached a set of large stained timber doors. Grabbing the handles, he pushed inward, revealing another chamber. The room reassembled a modern court room in shape but not in style.

This carpet alone is probably worth more than everything I own.

Kasey followed Clark up the aisle. They passed rows of empty timber pews. Passing through a small gate, Kasey spotted two desks, one on either side of the room.

Perhaps this is where the Arcane Council tries their criminal cases.

Agent Clarke addressed the room. "Members of the Council, I apologize for my tardiness. Miss Chase has not ever visited the Council Chambers and took longer than expected to arrive."

He bowed politely and then stepped back behind Kasey.

Who on Earth is he speaking to? The room is empty.

"Agent Clark, your diligence is always appreciated. Miss Chase, please step forward." An aging male voice called.

Kasey stepped forward, searching for the owner of the voice. It sounded like it was coming from above her.

As she looked up, she realized that what she had mistaken for the back of the room was actually an ornate wooden podium. It stretched from one wall of the chamber to the other. Seated high above her were seven figures in black robes with white horsehair wigs. At a glance, she guessed the raised stand must have been at least ten feet high. She had to crane her head up to see those seated behind it.

"Miss Chase, the Council has summoned you here in relation to a recent series of events, including those that took place at the Ninth Precinct police station here in New York."

Kasey strained to make out the speaker. A dour woman on the right-hand side of the bench was addressing her.

"Okay," Kasey replied. "I'm not sure what I can do to help you. Most of what I know is in the papers."

The woman slid her glasses down her nose and stared over the top of them at Kasey. "Miss Chase, we are aware that in the course of the attacks that substantial magical energy was released. We have reason to believe you were present and participated in such events. As you are well-aware, the use of magic in front of normals is a serious offense. One for which you have already received a warning, a warning which you appear to have violated in a matter of weeks. We've brought you here to address your flagrant disregard for the Council's regulations and determine whether or not a sterner punishment should be applied."

Kasey's heart beat faster as indignation rose. "First, you have brought me here on false pretenses. That is not at all what your agent intimated."

She glared at Clark, but his eyes were wide and his mouth agape. He looked just as surprised as Kasey.

"Secondly, just because I was at the heart of the attack doesn't mean it was my magic. I don't appreciate your assumption that it was me nor do I appreciate the presumption of my guilt."

"If you are not, please explain the events as you experienced them," a voice called from the center of the table. Kasey identified the speaker at once. It was Arthur Ainsley. "You have the floor Miss Chase. State your case."

Kasey considered just how much information she wished to give the Council. They might be the governing body of the magical community, but she was yet to have a single positive interaction with them or their enforcement agency. While the attack on New York posed a clear and present danger, Kasey was yet to be convinced the Council could be trusted. After all, the Shinigami army had crept into New York under their very noses.

"My case is simple. In the course of a recent investigation, I was tracking a killer. That killer happened to be a witch of considerable ability. In the course of pursuing her, she was run over and killed by a taxi. Her body was then taken to the Ninth Precinct for an autopsy and to garner any evidence that might lead us to her companion. As I conducted the autopsy, it became apparent that she had altered her appearance using magic."

There were murmurs from the raised bar.

Arthur's stern voice cut them off. "Using magic to assume another's form is a grave violation of our statutes. Those spells aren't even taught at the Academy anymore. I find it hard to believe you have encountered a witch capable of such magic. We haven't had a case of Identity Imitation for almost a decade."

Kasey nodded. "I was told as much when I called my mother. Before you get all up in arms, my mother is a witch. She's even registered with the Council. I believe you know her, Jane Stonemoore."

There was a series of whispers from behind the bench as the Council conferred with each other.

"Yes, that Jane Stonemoore. It may interest you to know the suspect I was investigating had a rather unique tattoo on her right wrist. Further research revealed it to be the mark of the Shinigami. The suspect I thought was a young woman, seems to in fact be a witch of considerable age, perhaps 70 or 80 years old."

"Miss Chase, if the Shinigami were in New York, we would know about it," another Council member asserted. "As acting head of the ADI, I can assure you we have detected no such thing."

The speaker was a young wizard sitting on the far-left hand side of the bench.

"Well, you'll have to forgive me for not taking your word for it, Mr...?"

"Sanders," the wizard replied.

"Well, Mr. Sanders, your information seems to be incomplete. Not only are the Shinigami here in New York, but they are also responsible for the death of your predecessor Cyrus Pillar."

This time the bench devolved into furious chatter. There was no attempt at whispering.

Arthur Ainsley picked up his gavel and beat it against the bench.

"Order. We will have order. Miss Chase, explain yourself at once."

"I intend to," Kasey replied. "You were there at the Gala, Arthur. You witnessed the attack and the senseless killing of all of those innocent people. I told you then that I thought I saw someone kill Cyrus. A waiter.

"You told me I was confused but when we conducted Cyrus' autopsy, the evidence was conclusive. He was killed by a pistol at close range from the side of the table occupied only by guests at the gala.

"The thieves were firing similar ammunition, 9mm rounds, but from very different weapons. Ballistics tests conducted with the other weapons in our possession indicated Cyrus was indeed murdered by another guest at the gala, not the thieves.

"We tracked down that killer. It was the Shinigami I mentioned earlier. They also orchestrated the attack on the Gala to conceal Cyrus's murder."

"Why would they do something like that?" Sanders demanded from the bench.

Kasey looked at the young wizard. "I'm not sure yet, but if I had to guess, I would say it was to throw the ADI into confusion while they plan their next course of action."

"You believe they are still here?" Sanders asked, his voice timid.

"One of them is," Kasey replied. "I understand there are always four Shinigami. No more, no less. One of them was run over on the street. Two of them died in the attack on the Precinct, and one of them, their master, remains at large. It seems they have plans for our city and after seeing them in action at the precinct, I can only wonder how many lives they plan to take."

"What..." Sanders began.

Arthur held up a hand to silence him. "Miss Chase, this is a very enthralling tale in theory, but do you have any evidence to support your outrageous claims?"

"I have the bodies of our police officers that were buried this week," Kasey replied. "I'm not making this up."

"Oh, but you could be," Arthur continued. "Those men were shot. None of the reports from survivors at the station refer to the use of magic or other unexplained phenomena. We know it occurred, but if the Shinigami were rampaging through your station, there would be far more evidence of their magic. I find it far more likely that your station was attacked, and in the chaos, you used your magic to save your own skin. I saw you try to do as much at the Gala. Will you deny it?"

"Not at all," Kasey replied. "I did consider using my magic, not just for myself but for the hundreds of other innocents who stood to lose their lives that night. So did you, if I remember correctly?"

The other members of the bench turned on Arthur.

"Indeed, I did, the subtle difference being my decades of experience doing so. I'm not a brash young woman who is not only un-educated in the use of her powers but also unregistered with the Council. Don't try to equate us. We are nothing alike."

"Well, that may be the case," Kasey replied, "but as you yourself have said, you have no evidence of anyone witnessing any magic during the attack on the Precinct, so your summoning me here and accusing me of it is wasting my time with baseless allegations.

"The Shinigami are the threat here, not me. I'm simply trying to do my job. Rather than wasting your time harassing me, why don't you find out why one of the Council was murdered and what the Shinigami have planned for this city.

If looks could kill, Arthur's glowering stare would have done so instantly. "Oh, we will, Miss Chase. In the meantime, you are to leave law enforcement of the magical community to us and stay out of anything pertaining to the Shinigami threat. Real or imagined, they are not to be trifled with. We won't have you bringing their wrath down on the city."

Kasey was trembling with indignation. "You're not putting this on me, Arthur."

Arthur chafed at the familiarity of Kasey's address. "That's enough, Miss Chase. I think we're done here."

Kasey looked up at the Council, all of whom had their eyes fixed on her.

"Oh, we are done, all right, but the Shinigami are not. When it comes to dealing with them, you are light years behind me. I'm 3 – 0. Try to keep up."

Kasey turned for the door.

"Kasey!" Arthur shouted after her.

His call fell on deaf ears as she stormed from the chamber.

CHAPTER 7

K asey burst through the doors leading out of the Council Chambers, causing both ADI agents to startle. She didn't even break her stride.

She simply reached out her hand. "Give me my gun!"

The ADI agents looked at each other, unsure of how to respond.

"I'm leaving. Now give me my gun, so I can get out of here."

Agent Clark exited behind her. "It's all right, agents, you can return her weapon. Miss Chase has finished with the Council."

The agent strode over to his desk, reached into it and retrieved the weapon, before handing it to Kasey. She snatched the gun from his hand and jammed it in her holster.

Then she reeled to face Clark. "Well, I'd say it's been a pleasure, but that would be a lie. See you... Well, I'm gonna be honest and say never would be my preference. I'll show myself out."

She turned and strode through the metal detectors. The machines went off, but she ignored them and made her way back to the elevator.

As she approached the elevator, they chimed. The doors parted, revealing the last person on earth she wanted to see: John Ainsley.

She huffed. "You have got to be kidding me. What are you doing here?"

John raised his hands defensively, "Whoa, Kasey, easy there. I heard you were in the building, meeting with the Council, and I thought I would check if you were alright."

"You don't have to check up on me, John." Kasey stepped into the elevator and punched the button for the ground floor.

The elevator doors slid shut.

"Look, Kasey, clearly you're upset about something," John said, "but I feel confident in saying that at least this time, it isn't my fault. Whatever happened with the Council has you upset. Why not tell me about it?"

"Why do you even care?" she asked. His attitude of entitlement had been an ever-present thorn in her side at the OCME. The greatest perk of being with the NYPD was that she no longer had to put up with him on a daily basis.

The elevator continued its ascent.

He put his hands in his pockets. "I don't know what I was expecting, but I sort of thought after our time at the gala and me quitting my job so that you could have yours back, I'd at least begun to make up for how I had treated you."

Her mouth dropped open. When the chief had indicated she was free to return to the OCME, he had not mentioned John at all.

Perhaps he didn't know.

It made sense. Sampson wouldn't have made the offer while Ainsley was still on staff, nor would she have had the clout to sack him. John had given up his job, so that she could have hers back. The selflessness was an unexpected turn.

"Don't look so surprised, Kasey. The only way I could make sure the OCME would take you back, scandal or no scandal, was to leave them shorthanded. Quitting my job meant that they would come looking for you. I made you a promise and I lived up to my word. Can we please put the past behind us and start over?"

She studied him intently. He certainly seemed sincere enough, and him resigning his job at the OCME was no small gesture. He'd spend just as long as she had working his way there.

"I guess so," she conceded, leaning against the elevator wall. "I'm sorry, John, I'm in a foul mood. It seems the Council is exactly the bureaucratic nightmare I expected them to be."

The elevator stopped, and its doors parted. Kasey stepped off the elevator into the bank's secured hallway. John was right behind her.

"What do you mean? What did the Council want from you?"

She stopped and turned to face him.

"It was because of the attack on the precinct. Dozens of police were injured or killed, but in amongst it all there was evidence of magic being used. The Council assumed it was me flaunting our sacred rules." Her voice dripped with sarcasm.

He nodded. "So, they dragged you down here for risking exposure and discovery of our world, right?"

"Yeah, that's pretty much it. Wasn't even me this time. And I still get blamed."

John glanced up and down the hallway to ensure they were alone. "Wasn't you? Who else could it be? I didn't know we had any other wizards at the Ninth Precinct."

Kasey shook her head. "The wizards weren't on our side. The group that attacked the station were hostile magic users supported by a handful of their acolytes armed with heavy weapons. They stormed the station and cornered me in the morgue."

John's eyes went wide. "What happened?"

"They tried to burn down the building with me in it. Fortunately for me, I survived, barely. Neither of them made it out alive. Unfortunately for me, with them both dead and their bodies incinerated, there isn't a whole lot of evidence for me to give in my defense. The Council thinks I was just using my magic for the hell of it. They're worried that someone at the precinct will find out."

John shuddered as Kasey recounted the attack. "And did they?" he asked.

"No," she lied without hesitation. "I was the only one down there, and after my last mistake and the Council's warning, I wasn't going to just go blasting away with magic in front of police officers. I may have skipped out on school but I'm not stupid."

"I never said you were," he said raising his hands in self-defense. "Killing a wizard even in self-defense, that's an impressive feat. Seems I got off lucky just a broken rib."

Kasey's eyes narrowed as they bored into him.

"Easy, it was just a joke," he insisted.

"You need to work on your delivery," she replied.

He nodded. "I'll see what I can do. It seems you're in a bit of a hurry to get out of here. What happened?"

She sighed. "You wouldn't believe me even if I told you, so why bother?"

"Try me," he insisted.

"Well, I told this to your father and the Council, but they all think I'm crazy. They told me to leave it alone, so the adults could handle it."

"You're kidding," John said backing away.

Kasey laughed harshly. "Well, that wasn't their exact words, but it was the gist of it."

"What did you tell them?" he asked.

She considered the question. With John's father being a member of the Council, she figured it was only a matter of time before he heard it for himself.

"Just that I believe there are genocidal wizards plotting the destruction of New York City. I know that Cyrus' death at the gala wasn't an accident. It was a carefully calculated murder designed to throw the ADI into chaos and confusion at a time when we need them the most."

John shook his head. "Just that, you say? So, nothing of any consequence then?"

"Not based on their reaction," Kasey replied. "They simply told me to leave it in their hands and not go near it."

John shifted his weight from one foot to the other. "So, what are you going to do?"

"What does it matter?" Kasey answered. "If I tell you that, you're going to tattle on me to the Council. I don't need them getting in my way. Until this morning, they had no idea what was going on. Even without their help, we've managed to track down and eliminate three of the four Shinigami that came to New York. Now only one remains. I'm not gonna wait for the Council to get around to doing something. Time is running out and he's stepping up his plan. If we don't move quickly, New York will never be the same again."

"Do you have any leads?" John asked.

"Not a great deal," Kasey admitted. "We've been one step behind them until the attack on the Precinct. After they lost three of their number, the Shinigami have gone quiet. I am tracking down a lead for someone who might be involved, but I don't know what part he plays. He might be working with the Shinigami or simply an unwitting pawn in their plan. Either way he is involved, I'm going to sit on him until I get something I can use. Problem is, it seems someone else is out to kill him and I'm not sure who or why."

"Anyone I know?" John asked.

"I doubt it," Kasey replied. "I'm working the case with the NYPD, but it seems there is no shortage of people who might want him dead.

"Is there money involved?" John asked.

"What do you mean?" Kasey asked

"How much is he worth? If he is loaded, chances are it's about the money. If he isn't, it's more likely to be one of the other deadly sins: lust, greed, jealousy, take your pick. Between them, they account for most of the deaths in the city. You know that though, you see it every day."

Kasey considered the insight and what she knew about the Langstrodes. From her conversations with Martin, it could easily have been any of those emotions. But there was no denying Langstrode had money. A lot of it.

"He is loaded," Kasey admitted. "Seems to have money for days and plenty of property throughout the city."

"Then that makes it easier," John replied. "Simply follow the money. Ask yourself who stands to gain the most from his death. They will be your most likely suspect. Work out anyone who might profit from his untimely death and get eyes on them. Sooner or later, one of them will lead you to what you're looking for."

Kasey nodded. John's advice certainly seemed to accord with Bishop's thoughts. Mrs. Langstrode had the most to gain. Ending her loveless marriage could easily be solved with Sal's untimely death. Not to mention the fortune that she would inherit. If it wasn't her, the yoga teacher might be overstepping his bounds.

"Thanks, John. I've got to hit the road, but you've confirmed what we were thinking, thanks."

"Glad I could help," John replied with a smile. "I'll see you around."

Kasey pushed open the security door leading back into the bank's lobby. Heading for the door, Kasey sucked in a deep breath and exhaled slowly. She wanted to walk off her frustration.

She hit the sidewalk, heading south on Broadway.

Thinking of her encounter with the Council, she bristled.

What a waste of time. Particularly when we have so little to spare.

Langstrode's death could occur at any moment and this little detour with the Arcane Council had wasted several hours that she just couldn't spare.

Hopefully Bishop or Vida have turned up something that can help.

As she strode down the busy street. Kasey began reviewing everything she knew about the attack. From her visions, she knew it devastated New York.

She had witnessed the explosions tearing apart the city. She had seen it from a dozen different vantage points. Each time, it showed chaos and destruction on a scale she'd never before witnessed.

She replayed each of the visions in her mind, searching for meaning in them. It was her most recent vision, witnessed from the top of the completed Park Avenue skyscraper, that had set her on her current course.

She had seen dozens of buildings splinter and collapse throughout the city. But 432 Park Avenue had stood untouched by the attack. There was something about the building she was missing. Somehow, the monolithic structure survived the attack. Kasey couldn't imagine how such a towering structure could endure while all around it others had fallen.

The building had a tiny footprint and yet towered 1400 feet in the air. It seemed impossible that it would remain unscathed.

What if the building itself is part of the attack? What if the Shinigami have altered it with their magic? Is that even possible?

The more she thought about it, the more it made sense. The only way she could see for such an impressive structure to remain intact, was if it was somehow immune to the magical onslaught about to be unleashed.

Such immunity might involve complicity with the attackers. Sal himself might be a party to the attack.

I need to tread more carefully around him. What if he knows who the Master is? Or worse still, what if the Master of the Shinigami plans to kill Sal and assume his identity? He could then twist the Park Avenue Development to suit his plot.

This Shinigami's ability to shape shift and wear any face they wished presented a multitude of options, each terrifying. One thing was clear: if the skyscraper at Park Avenue was involved in the attack, then Sal Langstrode's life being in danger was not a coincidence. Saving him might help thwart the attack itself.

A noise startled her. She jerked back, heart racing. When she realized it was her own phone ringing, her cheeks flushed.

Still a little jumpy. Who could blame me after what I've seen though?

She pulled her phone out of her jacket pocket. Recognizing the number, she answered it.

"Bishop, what can I do for you?"

"Where are you?" Bishop asked.

"I just finished at the Council. I'm on my way back to the station now."

"Don't bother, we've been digging into Mrs. Langstrode and I think it's time we had a chat with her. I'm about to head over. Are you able to join me?

"Sure can."

"Where are you?" Bishop asked.

"Heading south on Broadway. I'm on the right-hand side if you are heading with the traffic."

"Okay, head north and keep your eyes open. I'll be there in a moment."

"Sure thing." Kasey spun and began to head north instead.

A new thought filling her mind.

What have you been up to, Mrs. Langstrode?

CHAPTER 8

K asey and Bishop sat in the squad car on the corner of East Hundred and Second and Fifth Avenue. On both sides of the road, luxury apartments towered above them. Each building boasted spectacular views of Central Park. Even the cheapest of the apartments rented for more than four thousand dollars a week. As she peered up at them, Kasey could only imagine what it would be like to live on the Upper East Side.

"It's interesting to see how the other side live, huh?" Bishop asked.

"You're not wrong," Kasey replied. "I wish I lived next to Central Park. My evening run would be a heck of a lot more scenic than jogging through the ghettos."

"Oh, come on, Kasey." Bishop laughed. "It's not that bad."

Kasey drummed her fingers on the dashboard as they waited. "Perhaps not, but I'll say I have enjoyed being back at my parents, even if it is just for a few days."

Bishop turned a Kasey. "How is the insurance claim on your apartment coming along?"

"They're fighting it," Kasey answered. "They are saying it was arson, and let's be honest, they aren't wrong. But it was also fallout from criminal activity beyond my control, so I guess we'll see how it goes. Funnily enough, my policy doesn't cover werewolf serial killers, so I imagine I'll be at my folks for a while yet."

"Oh, well, it could be worse. You could live here and have your family out to kill you, like our friend, Langstrode."

Kasey laughed. "You're right. Compared to his, my problems look positively tame. I don't envy him. I remember how I felt with Danilo after me. It's pretty unsettling to know that somewhere out there, there is someone waiting, ready to kill you at the first opportunity."

"Speaking of Sal," Bishop replied. "There he is now."

She pointed across the road at where a cab had pulled up in front of the luxury apartments. Sal was getting out of the back seat.

"Hmm, seems like he didn't drive today. Maybe his car got booted for all its parking violations," Kasey wondered out loud.

"What do you mean?" Bishop asked.

"Oh, it's nothing. Just when I met him the other day, he was flipping out over a ticket. I get the feeling he's had more than a few of them."

Bishop laughed. "Oh, well, let's go see how he's doing. I called him about visiting his family for a chat. He insisted that he be present and until we have a little more to go on, we don't have a lot of other choices. It's not like we can just haul his wife down to the station without cause."

She popped her door and got out of the car. Kasey did likewise, then followed Bishop to the street corner toward Sal's house.

The whine of an engine speeding up drew Kasey's attention. With that many revs, it was clearly exceeding the speed limit. She glanced right to see a motorbike flying down Fifth Avenue. The bike slid through a red stoplight at the intersection of 103rd Street. Its rider was hunched low and wearing black motorcycle armor with a matching helmet.

A pit formed in her stomach.

Something isn't right.

Kasey reached for Bishop to warn her, but Bishop was already staring at the bike. As the bike sped toward them, all eyes, including Sal's, were drawn to it.

Bishop sprang into action.

"Sal, get down!" Bishop shouted, drawing her Glock.

Sal looked from Bishop to the approaching bike. Then he ducked behind the taxi he had just emerged from.

The bike screeched to a halt in the middle of Fifth Avenue. The rider drew a machine pistol and emptied it into the taxi. Bystanders screamed as bullets tore through the yellow paint, puncturing the body of the car. Pedestrians scattered away from the shooter.

Kasey focused her mind and considered bringing her magic to bear on the shooter. There were people everywhere, though. Passengers in cars all around the shooter had hunkered down. Stuck in traffic, they had nowhere to go. On the sidewalk, people were cowered behind trash cans and anything else they could find. There was no chance Kasey could intervene without dozens of potential witnesses watching her work magic. In the heat of the moment, she froze, unsure what course of action she should take.

Bishop did not.

With lives on the line, Bishop drew a bead on the shooter and fired, three shots in quick succession. The rider bucked as the bullets struck him, knocking him off his feet. The bike fell sideways as the rider was unseated.

"Kasey, check on Langstrode," Bishop said waving Kasey away. "I have the shooter."

Kasey turned and raced toward Sal. He was still hunkered behind the taxi. Fortunately, the rear wheel and the body of the taxi had stopped the bullets meant to end his life.

Reaching Langstrode, Kasey grabbed his arms and lifted him to his feet. "Are you okay? Did they hit you?"

Sal's lip quivered, not at all the bully he had first been when Kasey had met.

"Uh-uh," he stammered, struggling for words.

Kasey searched him for wounds but found none.

The entire incident had surprised her. She knew what she had seen in her vision: Langstrode tumbling through the air after being thrown from a building.

Watching a gunman try to kill him in broad daylight thirty feet from Central Park was not what she had expected.

Why didn't I see this?

"W-What happened to the shooter?" Sal finally managed, his teeth chattering.

"The shooter is down," Kasey replied. "Lucky for you, we were here. My partner is checking the body now. You stay where you are. I'm going to go check on her."

Sal simply nodded and leaned against the taxi for support. Kasey rounded the vehicle, then halted. A man was cowering in the driver's seat. Changing course, she opened the driver's door.

"Ah! Don't shoot," the driver pleaded, shakily putting up his hands in front of him.

The driver looked like he was in his fifties, a thin ring of grey hair lining his balding head

"Don't worry, I'm with the police. Were you hit?" Kasey asked as she searched the interior of the car. It seemed most of the bullets had slammed into the rear section of the vehicle. Only a single bullet had struck the driver side door, and as she examined the interior panel, she could see it hadn't made its way through the door.

"I'm fine," the driver answered, trembling.

"You may not have been shot, but I think you're in shock. Wait here for the paramedics. They will take care of you."

"What about my car? How do I explain this to my boss?" the driver asked.

"Don't worry about that," Kasey said. "It will all be in the police report. The report will take care of your boss and the insurer, but I need you to relax and wait for the paramedics. Everything will be okay."

The man nodded, taking short, deep breaths.

Kasey moved out into the traffic, weaving between the cars that had come to a standstill. The street had turned into a parking lot. Further down 5th Avenue, impatient drivers honked their horns, but she didn't have the time to respond.

She found Bishop crouched over the shooter's body. The shooter's legs were pinned underneath the back wheel of the motorcycle. An automatic pistol, the assassins weapon, lay on the street. Scattered around him were a dozen spent shell casings.

Bishop removed the shooter's helmet, revealing a man in his thirties. He had jet black hair, probably dyed, and a well-groomed mustache. Unfortunately for him, his motorbike armor did nothing against bullets. A pool of blood was slowly expanding underneath him. Kasey reached to check for a pulse.

"Don't bother, Kasey. He's already dead. With him shooting up the street like that, I couldn't take any chances. I had to put him down for the count."

"Did he say anything?" Kasey asked.

"Nothing at all. He was coughing up blood when I reached him. I think one of the rounds punctured a lung. He was dead in seconds," Bishop answered while searching the body.

"Find anything helpful?" Kasey asked.

"Nothing yet." Bishop made her way down to his pants, then halted over a lump in his hip pocket. Reaching in, she drew out the man's phone.

"A phone. It's not even locked. Amateur, seems our friend just took a call. We should be able to get something off that," Bishop said with a hint of excitement. "We at least need to bag the gun and the phone. I'll call it in, you get your kit."

She unhooked the keys for the squad car from her belt and handed them to Kasey.

Kasey took the keys and then ran to the vehicle. At the vehicle, she popped the trunk, found her crime scene kit, and hauled it out. Her heart was still racing. She kicked herself for freezing up, if it wasn't for Bishop, Langstrode would have been killed. Kasey shook off the thought, and kit in hand, she raced back to Bishop.

Bishop stood and tried to shoo the bystanders away. "Go on, folks, nothing to see here. Move it along. Let's get this traffic flowing again."

Placing the kit on the asphalt, Kasey crouched down and popped it open. Looking at the full Tyvek suit she paused.

I don't know that I have time for that.

Slipping on her latex gloves, she picked up the phone and slid it into an evidence bag before placing it in the kit. Next, she picked up the weapon. It was still where it had fallen when the shooter had gone down. At this point, it served little value as evidence. There would be no court case here. It was more important to secure the weapon so that it didn't pose any further danger to society.

She checked the chamber and the magazine both were empty before bagging the weapon and tucking it into the kit as well.

As she packed up her kit, two more police officers arrived.

"What's going on here?" One of the officers called to Bishop. "We're responding to a four-one-seven at this address."

"That's him," Bishop answered, pointing to the shooter. "He tried to gun down a person of interest in our current case. Unfortunately for him, we were here too. He's already dead. But we need you to secure the scene while we check on our victim. Could you help with that?"

"No worries, detective. We'll take the street, you see to your victim."

"Thanks, officers. Appreciate it." Bishop wiped her brow as she turned to Kasey. "Where's Langstrode?"

Kasey wandered toward the cab. "I left him behind the taxi. Don't worry, he didn't take any fire."

Bishop breathed a sigh of relief as she rounded the taxi, then halted. "Um, Kasey, if that's the case, where is he now?"

Kasey took two quick steps to catch up with Bishop and then realized Langstrode was gone.

"He was pretty shaken up. He must have headed upstairs to sit down," Kasey said, glancing around.

"Oh, inside?" Bishop asked. "You mean, inside to the wife we think is trying to kill him?"

Kasey saw Bishop's point. "Oh, crap. We better get in there."

"You're telling me," Bishop replied, then broke into a run.

Kasey hurried after her. They sprinted for the door only to find a doorman blocking the way.

"NYPD, we're going to need you to move," Bishop shouted.

A wrinkle of concern appeared by the man's eyes, but he remained firmly planted in the door. "What's going on here?"

"I need you to move out of the way," Bishop demanded. "One of your residents was almost gunned down on your doorstep. We have reason to believe he may still be in danger."

"Who?" the doorman asked.

"Sal Langstrode," Kasey answered.

The doorman stepped out of the way. "The Langstrodes are in the penthouse. The elevator on the right is already waiting."

"Thanks," Bishop answered, charging across the lobby.

Kasey hurried to keep up with her.

The lobby of the luxury apartments were richly furnished, but Kasey didn't have time to envy the décor as she followed Bishop past the concierge's desk and into the hallway lined with banks of elevators. The first elevator was waiting as the doorman had indicated. Bishop mashed the button on the wall panel and the elevator's doors parted.

Kasey and Bishop stepped onto the elevators. Kasey hurriedly pressed the topmost button. It had a gold embossed p for penthouse.

The aluminum doors closed, and the elevator hummed into motion.

Kasey studied Bishop. She was shifting her weight from one foot to the other as the elevator rose. Her hand hovered near her holster.

Kasey drew a deep breath, trying to calm her racing heart.

The elevator chimed, and the doors parted. Kasey stepped off the elevator, Bishop right behind, and found herself in a small lobby. The polished tiles shone as they caught the afternoon sun through the window.

At the other side of the room stood a single door. It was ajar. Raised voices carried through it and into the lobby.

"What was that, Cynthia? I tell you I'm coming home early, and there just happens to be a hitman waiting for me on my doorstep."

"Come on, Sal, you're being ridiculous. Why would I want you dead? It makes no sense at all. Where would you get such an absurd idea?" A high-strung voice replied.

Langstrode's voice bellowed a reply. "The police. They showed up at work the other day, telling me they had received a tip off that someone was organizing an attempt on my life. I thought there were insane until five minutes ago. How could you do this to me?"

Kasey and Bishop rushed across the foyer.

A third voice spoke up. "Come on, Sal. Put the gun down."

Kasey's heart skipped a beat.

Oh, no.

Bishop drew her Glock with her right hand as her left pushed the door open.

A woman, presumably Cynthia, stood in the middle of the room shaking. She was wearing a set of hot pink yoga pants and a white sportswear jacket. Beside her stood a man Kasey didn't recognize. He was wearing loose fitting green pants and a white singlet. He seemed to have an unnaturally olive tan that Kasey was sure came out of a bottle and not from the sun. His short brown beard was tapered to a point, and his hair was drawn back into a topknot.

He's either the yoga instructor or Robinson Crusoe.

All three of them whirled to face the door. On seeing Bishop, gun in hand, Sal didn't bat an eyelid. Cynthia and the yoga instructor were not nearly as collected. Cynthia's eyes bulged as she backed away slowly.

The yoga instructor was aghast. "Who are you?" He demanded.

Kasey's eyes scanned the lavish penthouse to Sal standing behind a mini bar. He had a glass of what looked like whiskey in one hand and a short stubby pistol in the other. The weapon was pointed directly at his wife.

"Shut up, Leith. You can Namaste out of this. It's bad enough that you're carrying out your torrid little affair under my roof, but the more you speak, the more I think the pair of you might be in it together."

"Sal, lower the gun," Bishop stated firmly. "The killer is dead, and you are safe. Put the gun down. Let's not do anything rash."

"Rash?" Sal shouted. "These two idiots just tried to kill me." His gun shook as he alternated between pointing it at Cynthia and Leith.

"That may be true," Bishop said, "but this isn't how we deal with it. We gather evidence and we put them in jail. If you shoot them, they will be dead but a jury of your peers will see you as nothing more than a jealous husband and a murderer. You will spend the rest of your life rotting in the cell. Do you really want that?"

Sal bit his lip as he considered Bishop's advice.

"Come on, Sal," Kasey added. "I told you we would watch out for you and we have. You're safe now. Put the gun down so that we can talk."

"You say that now, but for how long? What happens if they try again?" Sal said, shaking his weapon.

"That's going to be difficult for them, given they will be in our custody," Bishop replied.

"What?" Cynthia turned to glare at her. "You can't arrest us! We haven't done anything. What happened to innocent until proven guilty?"

"You've been watching too much TV, Cynthia. We don't need to prove you are guilty now. We can hold you for twenty-four hours while we gather the last of the evidence we'll need. Attempted murder is a messy business, particularly with your shooter dead. Unfortunately for you, you went cheap. A hit like that in broad daylight, if he was that sloppy here, I have no doubt once we dig into him, we'll find enough to press charges against the pair of you."

Cynthia's hands tightened into fists. "You can't do this to me! I'm innocent."

"That's for the jury to decide. Now sit down and shut up," Bishop commanded.

Cynthia collapsed angrily onto the cream couch.

"You, too," Bishop said, nodding at Leith. "On the couch beside her and keep your hands where I can see them".

Without a sound, Leith dropped onto the couch next to Cynthia.

Cynthia continued to shoot angry glares at her husband who was still aiming his gun at her. Leith's gaze was downcast. Leaning forward, he rested his head in his hands.

Bishop turned to Sal. "Alright, Sal, I'm going to need you to put down the weapon. As you can see, they are unarmed and no danger to you now. We are going to take them down to the station for questioning, but before we can do anything, you need to put that weapon down."

Sal looked at the pistol in his hand and then back at Bishop. His hand trembled, perhaps as he recalled what had happened to the assassin on the street. Bishop was a crack shot. If she could drop an assassin across a crowded street, then he didn't stand a chance standing fifteen feet away.

He lowered the weapon and placed it on the counter. "My apologies, detective. When I saw them both here, I didn't know how to react."

Bishop made her way over to the mini bar and secured the pistol. "Understandable, Sal, but you need to be careful. Otherwise, you'll land yourself in as much trouble as your wife. Target or not, you can't go around shooting people. Do you understand me?"

He slumped back against the counter and nodded. His eyes were tinged with red. Black bags had begun to form underneath them and his drooping lower lip spoke volumes concerning his condition. Kasey could empathize. After all, not too long ago, she had been in the cross hairs.

"Alright you two, come on downstairs," Bishop said, turning to Cynthia and Leith. "There's a squad car waiting. It's going to take you down to the station."

Leith lifted his head. "But I haven't done anything. I'm just a yoga instructor. I have no idea what's going on here."

Kasey raised her eyebrow. "When was the lesson scheduled for?"

"Three pm, the same as usual," Leith said.

Kasey glanced down at her watch. "So, you've been here for two hours and neither of you have worked up a sweat. I don't know about you, Bishop, but I'm having trouble seeing past that."

Bishop scanned the room. "No, Kasey, you're right. I think we all know that there is more going on here than yoga. The only real question is how much more. Kasey, could you help me out for a moment?" Bishop pulled her hair back out of her face.

"What's up?"

"That phone I gave you earlier, its call log showed that it received a call less than an hour ago. Would you mind pulling it out and giving that number a call? I was a little surprised that it wasn't a private number. Really gave me the impression we are dealing with amateurs."

Kasey placed her kit on the table and opened it. Still wearing gloves, she removed the evidence bag and then slid the phone free. She flicked to the call log.

Both Cynthia and Leith stared at the phone. Cynthia shuffled awkwardly on the couch, but Leith simply leaned back and folded his arms.

Kasey dialed the number. The penthouse was silent but for the phone in her hand. After several seconds, ringing echoed from somewhere nearby.

Kasey raised an eyebrow. "Isn't that interesting? The shooter's last call came from a phone in this room."

Both Cynthia and Leith began to look about madly.

"Don't even think about getting up," Bishop snapped, her weapon still in hand.

Kasey followed the ringing across the room to a glass door that led onto a balcony. At the base of the door was a knapsack. The ringing was coming from the knapsack.

Kasey picked up the bag and held it up. It had a garish peace sign dyed into it. Certainly not what she would have expected the well-dressed Cynthia to own. Leith, on the other hand, was looking decidedly uncomfortable.

Kasey opened the top of the knapsack and reached inside. It took only a moment to locate the phone, and it was still ringing. "Look what we have here. Who would have guessed it? Leith, looks like you're more than a yoga instructor, after all."

Leith leapt out of the seat. "I have no idea why that's ringing. I didn't call anyone."

Bishop leapt toward him, grabbed his arm, and twisted it. Holstering her weapon, she drew her cuffs. "Leith, you have the right to remain silent. Anything you say or do can and will be used against you in a court of law. You have a right to an attorney. If you cannot afford one, one will be appointed for you. Do you understand these rights as I have explained them?"

Leith sobbed as Bishop fastened the cuffs.

"Well, you have your answer," Cynthia said. "I can't believe you tried to kill my husband."

She shook her fist at Leith.

"Kill your husband?" Leith blubbered through the tears. "Don't give me that. You weren't thinking about your husband when we were in the shower earlier, were you?"

"What did you say?" Sal shouted, slamming his hand on the counter.

"Easy, Sal," Bishop warned. "We're going to take these two lovebirds down to the station and have a chat. In the meantime, we can't be sure that you are safe here. Come downstairs with us. There are some officers there. You can ride to the station with them, and we'll put you under a protective detail until we get this mess sorted."

Sal opened his mouth to protest but Bishop narrowed her eyes at him. "That wasn't a request."

"Fine, but I'm bringing the bottle," Sal answered, picking up the bottle of scotch off the counter.

Kasey popped both phones into the evidence bag and slung the knapsack over her shoulder. Bishop led Leith to the door.

"Come on, Cynthia," Kasey prodded. "It's time we all got to know each other a little better.:

Cynthia let out a derisive breath and stood up, avoiding Kasey's outstretched arm she followed Bishop and Leith to the door. Kasey and Sal were only a step behind.

As Kasey closed the door behind them, there was one thought she simply couldn't escape.

My vision showed two thugs throwing Langstrode off his building, not these two clowns and an amateur hitman.

If Cynthia or Leith had hired a gunman to kill Sal, it meant only one thing.

There was more than one person who wanted to see Sal dead.

CHAPTER 9

When they arrived at the station, Sal had a protective detail assigned to him whilst Cynthia and Leith had been placed in holding to stew.

The evidence may have been scarce initially, but with the suspects in hand and the shooter in a body bag, it began to mount quickly over the next several hours.

The shooter was identified as Anton Gunderson, a local thug with several minor convictions. He had been the chief suspect on two previous homicides. Unfortunately, both cases had fallen apart due to lack of evidence. With the Ninth Precinct's morgue being out of commission, his body was currently being examined by the ODME.

Kasey didn't really expect the autopsy to produce any useful information. After all, they knew he was the hitman and that he had been hired to kill Langstrode. His cause of death, also, was very apparent—three of Bishop's slugs were lodged in his chest.

More important than the evidence his body might yield was the evidence he may have left behind. Technical analysts were scouring the phone for any other proof that might confirm who had hired him. His phone records had been subpoenaed and search warrants had been authorized and executed on his current address as well as Leith's home, car, and yoga studio.

It appeared that when Leith wasn't doing home appointments on the Upper East Side, he operated a small yoga studio in Brooklyn. How he landed in Cynthia Langstrode as a client, let alone a lover, was yet to be determined.

What puzzled Kasey were their reactions when they were confronted. Cynthia vehemently denied the charges whereas Leith had been taken completely by surprise. After their conversation with Martin, and her earlier talks with Sal, Kasey had no doubt Cynthia might be involved. Certainly, her husband's untimely demise would be very convenient. It would allow her to pursue anything she wished, safe in the knowledge that her late husband's insurance policy and substantial estate would ensure she never wanted for anything for the remainder of her life. Kasey put her indignation and denial down to an act. An act that she was sure would crumble when the totality of the evidence was presented.

Leith was the unknown. Either he was an exceptional actor, or the poor yoga instructor had simply found himself in the wrong place at the wrong time. A pawn in Cynthia's plan to kill her husband. The call placed from his phone to the killer seemed just a little too convenient for Kasey's liking.

Then again, there was every chance that the hippie yoga instructor was a willing accomplice in Cynthia's plan. His own words confirmed their belief that the two were involved in an affair. Leith would not be the first lover who had resorted to violence to claim the affection of the woman he loved. Taking Sal's place presented a comfortable and considerable change in station. From dingy apartment and yoga studio in Brooklyn to a penthouse overlooking Central Park, Leith's rise would be meteoric.

What concerned Kasey the most, however, was that the scene that had unfolded with the shooter was nothing like what she had witnessed in her vision.

Was I just having an off day? Are my visions on the fritz? Is that a thing?

An execution in broad daylight was a far cry from seeing the developer thrown from the scaffolding of his own building. They may have thwarted today's killing, but Kasey couldn't shake the feeling in her gut that told her the worst was yet to come. Sal was still in danger. She felt it in her heart, and she had never had reason to doubt her visions before. They had all come to pass eventually. If she had seen Sal thrown from the side of his building, then it would happen. If not today, then eventually. Whoever had concealed themselves behind the sheet had a plan for him. One that would not be deterred or dissuaded by money.

Her mind flitted back to the chief's words about Langstrode's dealings. Throwing the developer off his own building certainly felt personal. Kasey made a mental note to follow up with Vida and see if he had turned up anything on Langstrode's past business partners. Kasey hoped Vida's search might yield further suspects.

Kasey sat in the bullpen of the Ninth Precinct waiting for Bishop, who had been rushing around madly since they had returned to the station.

With Cynthia and Leith in custody, Bishop wanted all the evidence she could get before the two were released and had a chance to erase it. What Bishop was truly hunting for was a piece of evidence that would link the two undeniably to the shooter. The call placed from Leith's phone was a good start, but more would be required. They also needed to link Cynthia to the attempt on her husband's life.

They needed to be able to convince a jury beyond all reasonable doubt, then the Upper East side murderess and her yoga instructor would get what they deserved. Kasey picked up her pen and drummed it on the desk.

While she waited, another thought crept back to her mind. The decision to stay at the Ninth Precinct or return to the OCME. The chief's deadline had already passed, and Kasey still had no idea which she should choose. It felt like a betrayal of her boss to stay at the Ninth Precinct, but Kasey couldn't deny she enjoyed being on the front lines. She'd learned so much in the brief time she had been working with Bishop. The thought of going back to the quiet and uneventful morgue at the OCME just seemed dull by comparison.

There were also the resources of the Ninth Precinct. With Bishop and Vida now aware of the attack, and her secrets, Kasey was able to work unmolested as she fought to prevent the destruction of her city.

Each day it drew nearer, and she was still missing crucial keys. While she knew who lay behind it, how and where the attack would unfold remained a mystery. If she wanted to solve that and save the city, she needed to be able to move about, not be locked in a basement doing autopsies all day, every day.

Her thoughts turned to John. Weeks ago, she'd been responsible for cracking three of his ribs and still she found him creeping back into her thoughts from time to time. Him throwing himself on his sword to allow her to go back to her old job had certainly done a lot to improve her opinion of him. His thoughts on the case had reinforced Kasey's convictions that they were on the right track.

"Follow the money." That's what John had said.

Vida was still digging for answers, but Langstrode's life hung precariously in the balance.

With Langstrode still in protective custody in the station, Kasey decided to go to the source for the answers she needed. If anyone knew who would gain from Langstrode's death, it would be Sal himself.

Kasey got up off the desk and headed to the staircase. The third floor had a lounge where Langstrode and his protective detail were holed up. He had not been thrilled at the prospect of not being able to work and had set up shop in the lounge to try to salvage what was left of his working day.

Kasey ran up the stairs and hit the landing for the third floor. Pulling open the door, she found herself looking into the lounge. The officers at the table startled, then caught her gaze and relaxed.

"Sorry to startle you boys. I just have a few quick questions for Mr. Langstrode."

The officers nodded.

"No worries, Kasey," one of them said. "He's over there on the couch."

Kasey approached Langstrode, who was leaning over his laptop set up on the coffee table, typing away.

"Miss Chase, what can I do for you?" he asked as he stopped typing and looked up at her.

"I have a question for you, Mr. Langstrode."

He leaned back into the sofa. "Well, with what you and Bishop did for me today, I'll see what I can do to answer it for you. Fire away."

Kasey nodded. "Your current project, 432 Park Avenue...It's an impressive building."

Langstrode smiled. "Indeed, it is. When completed, it will be the tallest residential building in the city. It will also have one of the greatest height-to-building footprint ratios of any building ever constructed. It's a marvel of engineering. One that will allow me to leave a permanent legacy on our city skyline."

"The site..." Kasey continued sitting on the edge of the couch. "Is there anything special about it. Why did you choose Park Avenue?"

Langstrode smiled. "Truth be told, the site itself wasn't my decision. The land was owned by another who approached me to see if I would be able to help him develop it. The building is a joint venture.

"After all, a building of that magnitude is beyond even my means. If I had worked three lifetimes, I wouldn't have amassed enough capital to construct it."

"So, the building wasn't your idea?" Kasey asked intrigued.

"Not at all, Miss Chase, but I was more than happy to accept the project. The building will be the envy of all who visit the city. Apartments will have panoramic views of the city, from river to river and all of Manhattan. "

"I see." Kasey nodded. "So, your partner, you mind telling me who it is?"

"I don't see how that's relevant," Langstrode replied.

"Well, if all you've said is true, your project at Park Avenue will redefine the city. We are trying to protect your life and we are interested in any one who might have a vested interest in it ending."

"You have my wife in custody, so the threat to my life is over right?"

The voice inside Kasey's head screamed, no. She could hardly tell the developer about her vision, though.

"Well, we are taking every precaution just in case. The amateur hitman was hardly the sort of individual our informant would have been listening in on. We are protecting against the possibility that there might be other attempts on your life. We're just trying to cover all our bases."

Sal crossed his arms. "Well, you needn't worry about my business partners. First, I have a nondisclosure agreement in place, so I can't reveal my investor's identity. Second, they have no interest in seeing me dead. My name on this building doubles its value. On the Upper East Side, Langstrode still means something.

"My apartment buildings are some of the most sought after in the city. Killing me serves no purpose. In fact, if anything, it diminishes the value of their investment. They would need another developer to finish the project and the finished apartments would go for a far lesser price, particularly in the wake of my untimely death. It's not a good look for a project when the developer dies part way through its construction. People are superstitious, you know."

He made a good point but his lack of willingness to disclose the identity of his investors piqued Kasey's curiosity.

"You sure I can't persuade you to tell me who else is involved," Kasey asked.

Langstrode shook his head. "No chance at all. The NDA carries a penalty of ten million dollars. I'm not willing to take that big a bath just to indulge your curiosity. If someone else is out to kill me, you're barking up the wrong tree."

He reached for the coffee mug resting beside his laptop.

"Well, thanks for your time, Sal. I appreciate it. You stay here, where it's safe. We'll let you know once we have any more information.

Sal nodded, and Kasey stood up to make her way back to the bullpen. As she descended the stairs, she made a mental note to have Vida dig deeper into the investors. The more Sal did to conceal their identity, the more curious she became.

As she emerged from the stairwell, she almost ran into Bishop.

"Hey, Kasey, there you are. I've been looking for you."

"Sorry, I popped up to check on Langstrode to ask him a few questions."

"Anything interesting?" Bishop asked.

"Not yet. I just wanted to know a little more about the project he was working on. I'm trying to work out why someone would want him dead. I haven't got anything yet, but I'll keep you informed. Vida is doing some digging at the moment. How about you?" Kasey asked.

Bishop smiled. It was something of a rarity, and that grin could mean only one thing: she'd found something.

"Oh, yes, Kasey, we got them." Bishop answered, wringing her hands together.

"What did you find?" Kasey asked, following Bishop to the Bullpen.

"The officers that searched Leith's car found twenty thousand dollars tucked under the seat in a brown paper bag. No one keeps that kind of cash in their car for good reasons. Clearly he was planning on a pay off after the fact. He's as guilty as Cynthia.

I'm sure the idea was Cynthia's, but the execution seems to have the yoga instructor written all over it. Let's take a run at them and see what happens."

"Interrogation?" Kasey asked.

"You got it in one," Bishop said pointing to the interrogation rooms. "They have been stewing in separate rooms for hours. I'm thinking we should take a run at the instructor first. See if we can get him to break, then use his testimony to bring down Cynthia. What do you think?"

"Sounds like a plan. What do you want me to do?" Kasey asked as she followed Bishop to the interrogation rooms.

Bishop reached for the door handle and flashed Kasey a small grin.

"Nothing at all. Just sit back and enjoy the show. Let me know if you see anything interesting."

Bishop winked at Kasey and pushed open the door.

CHAPTER 10

K asey followed Bishop into the interrogation room. The room was stark, intentionally so. A single steel table dominated the center of the room. One wall was occupied by a one-way mirror, where observers could watch proceedings without being seen by the suspect.

Leith was sitting, bent over the table, his head resting on his arms. He had seen better days.

"Leith Carson," Bishop announced as she walked around the table. "Thirty-five years of age. No previous criminal record. Currently being detained on one count of conspiracy to commit murder. Mr. Carson are you with us?"

Leith lifted his head off the table. His face was red, his eyes swollen and puffy. He had not been doing well at all. A small puddle of dried tears had left smears on the otherwise clean table.

"I'm telling you I had nothing to do with that shooting." Leith whimpered. "I'm a yoga teacher, not a murderer, for heaven's sake."

"Come now, Leith, we all know better than that. Don't sell yourself short. You may be a yoga teacher, but you're also having an affair with Cynthia Langstrode. Punching well above your weight there, aren't you?

"Unfortunately for Mr. Langstrode, your little affair and subsequent greed almost got him killed today. If we hadn't shown up when we did, he would have been dead, and you would have been facing a very different set of charges."

Leith flopped back in the chair. "How many times do I have to tell you? I didn't try to kill him. Why would I do something like that? It makes no sense at all."

Kasey chimed in. "It's pretty simple actually, Leith. You start spending time in an Upper East Side apartment, nice views, lovely neighborhood, not to mention Cynthia. Sure, she might be a few years older than you, but let's be honest, she's a stunner.

"You start to get a little comfortable with the lifestyle and after a few months, you think, Hang on a minute. The only one standing between me and living this cushy lifestyle 24/7 is that inconvenient husband of hers. Not to worry, hitmen aren't nearly as expensive as you thought they were."

"That's right," Kasey added. "A brown paper bag full of cash later, you have the life you always wanted. No more being broke in Brooklyn. You can live the high society life with Cynthia. How are we doing?"

Leith shook his head. "You have it all wrong. Sure, I was having an affair with his wife, can you blame me? What red-blooded man would have said no to that? She pays me five times what any other client does, and I get a booty call too. It's fantastic, or at least it was until all this happened. I was happy with how things were. Murdering her husband to move in with her? That's crazy. Deep down, she is a piece of work. I'd be worried that I'd be next. I've heard her talk about her husband. I wouldn't be keen to take his place."

Bishop folded her arms. "So, what you are trying to tell me is that Cynthia is responsible for today's shooter and that you had no part of it? Is that right, Leith? Because, Leith, I'm having a few problems believing that."

"Yes, that's exactly what I'm saying." Leith leaned forward, trying to shake his hands for emphasis but the handcuffs gave him little room to move.

Bishop plowed on. "The first problem is this, the call to our killer's phone, only an hour before the hit, came from your phone. You saw it yourself in the apartment. We called the number. It was yours. Our technical analysts are working through both phones as we speak, but we already know that it was made from your phone. Explain that to me."

"I didn't make that call, detective. It may have come from my phone, but I didn't make it."

"Then who did, Leith?" Bishop asked.

"It must have been Cynthia," Leith said. "An hour before you all showed up, we were in the shower. Cynthia got out before me. She must've made the call while I was finishing up and then put it back in my bag. I know it was on the table before I got in the shower, so someone moved it and it wasn't me. I left it on the table with my keys when I arrived."

Bishop's eyes narrowed on Leith. He was like a deer caught in the headlights. Kasey recognized the look in her partner's eyes. Bishop was the hunter, ready to take the killing shot.

"If that's true, Leith, how do you explain this?" Bishop asked as she tapped the evidence bag on the table.

"What's that?" Leith asked, looking through the plastic to the brown paper bag within it.

"Twenty thousand in cash. We found it under the passenger seat of your car. That's a lot of money for anyone, let alone someone that claims to be broke in Brooklyn, wouldn't you say? Where did the twenty thousand dollars come from? You must teach one hell of a lesson for someone to pay that much cash. The fact that it was tucked into a paper bag in your car is also suspicious."

Bishop stood up and stretched. "More important than all of that, though, is that it is an identical amount to what was deposited in our shooter's bank account a week ago. What was the deal, Leith? Half upfront and half when the job was done? I've gotta give it to you, it was clever to use cash, a lot harder to trace than if you'd simply pulled it out of your bank account. It must have taken you a while to put that much together."

Leith stared at the cash, eyes wide. "Detective, you have it all wrong. I'm being set up. I've never seen that much cash in my life. If I had twenty grand, I wouldn't have wasted it on a hitman. I would have moved out of my crappy apartment and paid the outstanding rent on my studio. That's not my money. I don't care where you found it."

"You should care, Leith. A jury is going to care. The call from your phone, the cash in your car. Right now, you are more than an accessory—you are our prime suspect."

"Prime suspect? I shouldn't be involved at all. I'm being set up and you should be able to see that as clear as day," Leith protested

"If you've been setup, explain the money to us," Kasey replied. "Where did that come from."

"It has to have been Cynthia," Leith said. "I haven't had anyone else in my car for weeks. I picked her up from the salon today and took her home. She must've planted the cash knowing what was going to happen. Can't you see? When I didn't buy in to her discussions to get rid of her husband, she carried it on without me. Now I'm her scapegoat."

He slumped in the chair, his cuffed hands resting on the table. He was defeated.

"If it wasn't you, Leith, give us something we can use against her," Bishop said. "There is no need for both of you to go down for her crime. Did she text you about her plans? Do you have anything at all we can use?"

Leith pondered on the question, and then shook his head. "No, she never mentioned it in our texts. Just after we, you know. It was pillow talk. She'd say things like, 'Wouldn't it be great if every day was like this?' She said she wanted to be with me, that we had a bright future together. She would complain about him all the time. Told me she'd approached a divorce lawyer but that it hadn't gone the way she wanted it to. Wouldn't surprise me if she was trying to kill him so she could keep everything for herself."

"She didn't say anything about what she had planned?" Kasey asked. "She never indicated when this bright future might begin?"

"I'm sorry, officers. I have given you everything I can think of. I just got caught in the wrong place at the wrong time."

Bishop leaned over the table. "Well, Leith, we would love to believe you, but right now the evidence is not in your favor. We need to have a little chat with Cynthia. If you remember anything else, you let us know."

"So, I'm free to go?" Leith asked hopefully.

Bishop shook her head. "Afraid not. Until we get to the bottom of this, you are still our lead suspect. We will be holding you for twenty-four hours, at which time we'll reassess our evidence and decide what charges will be pressed and against whom."

"Twenty-four hours?" He looked around. "What am I meant to do until then? Just sit here?"

"Indeed. Get comfortable. It's going to be a long night." Bishop replied.

Kasey rose to her feet as Bishop turned and opened the door. Together, they stepped into the hall. Bishop closed the door behind them.

Kasey looked down the hall to interrogation room two. Contrary to expectation, the doors were open.

"What on earth? Who is in there speaking to Cynthia?" Kasey asked.

Bishop saw the door and picked up her pace.

They entered the room to find a man standing by the table. He was clean-shaven with slicked back hair. His suit was tailored, an expensive cut, Italian by the look of it. A black leather briefcase rested on the table beside him.

The vein in Bishop's neck seem to bulge reflexively, and her face turned red. It became apparent Bishop was familiar with their visitor.

Ignoring Bishop, the man reached out his hand to shake Kasey's.

Kasey looked at Bishop, unsure what to do, the Detective was scowling.

When Kasey didn't take his hand he simply withdrew it and smiled, the kind of wired smile that showed two perfect rows of teeth.

"Hello, I am Wayne Dichenzo, of Dichenzo, McBryde, and Foxx, and you are?"

"Kasey," she replied, not sure what to make of the visitor.

She couldn't help but notice Cynthia was wearing a satisfied grin, not at all the appearance of a woman waiting to be convicted for an attempt on her husband's life.

"Lovely to meet you, Kasey," Wayne said. "I didn't know Detective Bishop was mentoring a new detective. I would have thought she'd set a better example. Refusing a suspect their phone call and denying them their representation is not a pattern of behavior worthy of emulation. You'd do well to remember that. I'm surprised Bishop hasn't learned from our last soiree. When the Langstrode's didn't return home, the manager gave me a call. He thought they might need my services."

Bishop waved her hand dismissively. "No one denied anyone anything, Wayne. Your suspect has been detained as a lead suspect in the attempted murder of her husband. It occurred only hours ago. We're well within our rights."

Wayne smiled. "Oh, I think not, detective. You're right my client has been detained and has been here for several hours. What we are not in agreement on, is the fact that she is a suspect, lead or otherwise. I'm informed that you have no evidence whatsoever linking her to this supposed murder attempt, other than the drunken ranting of her husband who has clearly been traumatized by the day's events. Hardly a reliable basis for such outrageous allegations."

Bishop balled up her fist. Edging closer to the table, she leaned on it, probably to keep from punching Wayne's smug face.

"Supposed murder? Her hitman tried to gun down her husband in broad daylight on Fifth Avenue. It's a miracle more people weren't injured. As for evidence, the shooter may be dead, but we have little doubt that the money trail will lead back to your client. After all, she stands to gain the most from a husband's death and she was having an affair."

"That is baseless rhetoric and inadmissible in court, Bishop. You know that. Besides, I understand you have a suspect in custody who has already been linked to the killer. Do you not have evidence of a call he placed? It seems you already have what you need. Unless you have something more on my client I'd recommend you release her, or I will ensure we file a suit for harassment."

"What a load of crap," Kasey replied.

"Not at all. You can't detain a suspect without sufficient evidence, of which you have none," Wayne said. "We have an army of lawyers. We will bury you in so much paperwork, it'll take you the rest of your life to dig yourself out. Either find some evidence and press charges or release my client. Those are your choices. Shouldn't be too hard. Gathering evidence is your job after all, isn't it?"

Kasey pondered on a quick retort but found herself coming up short. No wonder Bishop hated this snake.

Bishop sighed, rounding the table, and drew out her keys. Slowly, she began to unlock Cynthia's handcuffs.

"What are you doing?" Kasey asked.

"We don't have enough yet to hold her," Bishop replied as she looked down at Cynthia.

Cynthia made no effort to hide her amusement.

"Don't be smug, Cynthia. I said yet. Kasey and I have closed more homicides in three weeks than most detectives do in three months. You're guilty as sin and it's written all over your face. Sooner or later, we'll find what we need. Enjoy your freedom while it lasts. Don't leave town."

Cynthia stood up and flashed a smile at Wayne. "Oh, I have no intention of leaving town, detective. After all, I'm innocent. Why would I leave town?"

Wayne gestured for the door, and Cynthia sauntered out of the room.

Picking up his briefcase, Wayne turned to Bishop. "When my clients ask to speak with their lawyer, you would do well to allow them their rights, detective. I don't want to have this discussion again."

"For the record, Wayne, she didn't ask for a lawyer until we began grilling her accomplice, so get of your high horse. Sooner or later, she'll be back here."

"I hope so, detective," Wayne replied. When Bishop's brow wrinkled in confusion, he continued, "More billable hours. In the meantime, you two have a great day."

Wayne disappeared through the door and out into the station.

Bishop slammed her hand on the table. "I can't believe the nerve of that guy. Of all the dirt bag criminal lawyers in the city, I like Wayne Dichenzo the least."

"Sounds like you two have history?" Kasey asked.

"It's not like that," Bishop answered. "Their offices are only three blocks away. Every time we arrest an East Sider for anything, doesn't matter whether it's possession or attempted murder, Wayne rides to their rescue. Seems to be the one number they all have on speed dial.

"He is responsible for more wealthy dirt bags evading the law than all other lawyers in the city combined. He's made his career out of opposing the work we do. We need to make sure our case is airtight. One bubble, one mistake, one chink in our armor and Wayne will find it. We need a concrete link between Cynthia and the shooter and we need it sooner rather than later."

"Then what do we do?" Kasey asked. "We can't just let her go free. She will just wait until the heat dies down and try to kill him again. Next time, we may not be there to save him."

"I know. We aren't just going to drop it, but we need more substantial evidence. Cynthia has done a good job of setting Leith up as the fall guy. She knew if things went sideways, she could just throw him to the dogs and it looks like that's precisely her plan. Unless we can get more out of Leith or find something that Cynthia left behind, she's going to walk."

"So, you believe Leith then?" Kasey asked, leaning on the desk.

Bishop nodded slowly. "I'm beginning to. The evidence mounting against him is a little too convenient. At first, I thought he might have been a lovestruck fool doing her bidding. Now I'm starting to think, he just had sex on the brain and Cynthia used him and framed him for the murder.

"At least, that's what I'm thinking at the moment. You go speak to Langstrode. Let him know that his wife is out of our custody. Sprung by their lawyer. Perhaps Sal can put some pressure on Dichenzo to drop the case. Without the money, Wayne won't give a damn about Cynthia. In any case, he should know that home isn't safe. We'll keep him here with his protective detail, so we can watch out for him."

"What are you going to do?" Kasey asked.

"I'm done for the day. I need to get out of here and blow off some steam. I think I'll head down to the pool and do a few laps."

"A swimmer, I wouldn't have pictured that," Kasey replied.

Bishop shrugged. "I've gotta do something to keep fit. I hate running, particularly in the winter, whereas the pool is at least heated. I can swim all year long and it feels great."

"Fair enough. I'll have a word to Sal then I'll head home myself. Enjoy your swim!"

"Night, Kasey," Bishop replied as she tidied up her desk.

The last few weeks had been so busy, Kasey had barely had a chance to hit the gym. Bishop's diligence brought on guilty pangs over her neglect.

I have more important things to do right now.

Hitting the stairs, she made her way back up to the lounge. When she reached the third floor, she found Langstrode on his feet, pacing. His protective detail was still sitting where Kasey had found them earlier.

Tough shift, boys?

"What's up?" Kasey asked, letting the door close behind her. "You're wearing out the tiles."

He stopped and looked up at her. His hands were shaking. "I'm sorry. I can't help it. The stress of today is starting to get to me. Being cooped up in this room isn't helping at all. I need to get out. I need a drink and I need to relax."

"What happened to the scotch?" Kasey asked.

"Finished. There wasn't much left when I started. It didn't last long."

"I know it's not easy. Believe it or not, a few weeks ago, I was exactly where you are now. A psycho was trying to kill me, and I was stuck here in the station. It's no way to live but you need to be patient. Until we catch whoever is responsible and put them away, your life is in very real danger. You saw that today. We can protect you in here, far better than we can out there."

"It's my wife and that yoga instructor. You already have them in custody. I don't see why I need to stay up here. Just charge them and let me go home."

Kasey approached him. His hair was tussled, and small creases had formed beside his lips from frowning.

"It's not that easy. The evidence we have does point to the yoga instructor, but we don't have anything linking your wife to the attempt on your life. Something that your lawyer was eager to point out, right before he had your wife released."

Langstrode's eyes went wide. "Released? What do you mean?"

"I mean, your hotshot lawyer just showed up and forced our hand. Some guy called Wayne Dichenzo. I don't know him, but Bishop seemed fairly familiar with his work. Apparently, your building manager called him. Well, we didn't have enough evidence to hold her, so we had to let go. So, the station is about the safest place you can be right now. If you think it's your wife that's out to kill you, you're safer in here than out there with her."

"That son of a..." Langstrode caught himself just in time. "Kasey, can you excuse me? I need to make some calls."

"Anything I can help with?" Kasey asked.

Sal shook his head. "No, I need to call my daughter and warn her not to go home. If Cynthia will try to kill me, Alicia isn't safe either. In the event that something happens to me, Alicia and Cynthia have equal shares in my estate."

Kasey nodded. She found it interesting that Sal hadn't said anything about Martin. Clearly his son's comments about their relationship hadn't been an exaggeration. Kasey decided to test the water anyway.

"You mentioned a couple of calls? Who is the other?" Kasey asked

"Wayne. I need to remind that pencil pusher who he works for. Then I'm going to have a chat to a divorce lawyer. I don't think I'll have any trouble getting a judge to see this as irreconcilable differences."

Sal pulled out his phone and Kasey left him to it.

She turned to the officers watching Sal. "Hey, guys, you know how these one-percenters like to do whatever they want. He's not going to want to stick around in here, so keep an eye on him, make sure he doesn't get in any trouble."

The officer, a young man in his thirties, smiled. "Don't worry, Kasey, we've got him. He's not going anywhere."

The elevator doors parted, and Kasey stepped inside. Her hand hovered over the button for the ground floor. She glanced at her watch and realized it was nine o'clock. She still hadn't given the chief an answer about her plans. The NYPD or the OCME. It was a tough choice to make, one that she had been taking turns agonizing over and avoiding all day.

She took a deep breath and punched the button for the fourth floor.

Time to see the chief.

CHAPTER 11

K asey stepped out of the elevator onto the fourth floor and came face-to-face with Chief West. The chief looked up and stopped in his tracks.

"Kasey, it's good to see you. I was actually coming looking for you."

"I know, chief. I'm sorry, we got a little caught up downstairs. I meant to talk to you earlier, but time got away from us."

The chief nodded. "Have you decided what you would like to do?"

His steely eyes seemed to bore into her soul.

"I have," she said.

No matter how grateful she was for her old boss and everything that she had done, there were more important considerations.

Something was coming to New York City. If Kasey was to stand a chance of stopping the attack, it would be with the resources of the NYPD at her side. She couldn't afford to run away to the OCME.

Turning a blind eye and just hoping for the best did not sit well with her at all. She'd run away from her visions before and that had got her nowhere. In fact, it almost got her killed when the assassin Danilo Lelac had come after her.

Now I'm running toward them.

"Don't keep me waiting, Kasey. I've got places to be," the Chief said.

"I want to stay," Kasey blurted. "Don't get me wrong, I love the OCME. Dr. Sampson was a hero to me, but I feel like the work I'm doing here with Bishop is even more important. Even now, we're fighting to save someone's life. I don't know that I can ever go back to the OCME. I don't think I would even want to. I'd love to stay here, if you will have me."

The chief smiled. "I wouldn't have it any other way. You and Bishop have proved unstoppable. I want to keep you two together and closing cases. We'll have to get you transferred to the Department full-time. Officially, you will be a medical examiner working under Dr. Katri, but we'll ensure your duties are flexible. You'll spend most of your time as a crime scene technician working beside Bishop.

"Evans is still away on leave, and he and Bishop didn't get along anyway. I'll call the OCME tomorrow and let her know. As for you, carry on as you were. We can't have Sal Langstrode killed on our watch." The chief pressed the button for the elevator and the doors parted.

"Mind if I share your ride?" The chief asked.

"I'm just heading down to the morgue," Kasey replied. "I may as well give Vida the good news now."

The chief pressed the button for the ground floor. "Ah, yes, speaking of, I've completed the requisition process and the renovations should begin next week. We'll have our own morgue back up and running before you know it."

The elevator came to a halt and the doors opened. As the chief stepped off the elevator, he turned to Kasey. "Try not to destroy this one, would you? The city is really busting my balls over the repair bill."

Kasey nodded. It was a good thing the chief had no idea just how true that statement was. The doors closed, and Kasey pressed the button for the basement. Moments later, the door parted once more, and Kasey found herself wandering down the familiar hall to the battered remnants of the morgue.

The burnt-out shell of the morgue was just as she had left it. The white board dominated the now empty room, and the light in Vida's office was on. As she had hoped, the doctor had not yet left for the evening.

Kasey approached the office and found Vida bent over his keyboard, staring at his screen. His desk was littered with paperwork. So fixated was he, that he did not notice her approach. She crept across the room, ensuring she didn't make a noise.

When she was behind Vida, she bent down until her mouth was mere inches from him. "So, whatcha doing?"

He jumped a mile. She slid back to avoid being hit by his flailing arms.

As the chair rolled out, Vida found his feet. "Kasey, what are you doing? You almost gave me a heart attack."

He patted himself on the chest as he tried to contain himself.

Kasey chuckled. "Sorry to sneak up on you, it was just too good an opportunity. I couldn't pass it up."

Vida drew in a deep breath. "You're going to be the death of me. If it's not witches trying to kill me in my own morgue, it's you scaring me to death when I'm not watching. Feel my heart, it's going to explode. You shouldn't sneak up on a man like that."

"Relax, Vida," she replied as she slid his chair back to him. "You'll be surprised what you can live through. I like to think I am just expanding your horizons."

"Expanding my horizons?" He said pointing to the blasted remnants of his morgue. "Last week, I had to stab a man with a scalpel just to stop him from obliterating you with magic. There is a sentence I never thought I would say out loud. I think you can consider my horizons amply widened, thank you very much." He sat back in the chair.

Kasey rested her hands on his shoulders and gave him a light massage. "So, what had you so caught up in the first place? Find something interesting?"

He picked up his pen off the desk and began to tap it against the edge of the table. "It depends what you consider interesting. I've been digging through the documentation behind Langstrode's construction project, trying to get an idea of just who he might be in business with."

"What did you come up with?" She asked, stepping to his side, her interest piqued.

"Well, the corporation that actually owns the land is a private company called Genesis Holdings. I've been digging into the company, but there isn't a whole lot of information on them. Simply a one-page website about reshaping the New York City skyline.

"There are a few pictures and plans about the Park Avenue project and a sales page for luxury apartments, but there is precious little else in the way of information about those who run the company. They have little to no trading history and only formed up as a company about three years ago. It was just before they purchased the property from the bank.

"The owners of the previous building had defaulted on their mortgage during the GFC and the banks seized control of the old apartments and sold them at auction.

"According to Sotheby's, the land was bought by a phone-in bid. They never met the purchaser in person, and a law firm on the East Side, Nelson Brothers, acted for them in the settlement. Whoever Genesis Holdings are, they are going to great lengths to conceal their identity."

Kasey sighed. "I tried to get some more information out of Langstrode, but he wouldn't have a bit of it. Said he had a non-disclosure agreement that carried a ten-million-dollar charge for non-compliance."

"He wouldn't tell you, even though someone is trying to kill him," Vida said, turning back and forth in his chair. "I think it's safe to say your hunch is right. There is more going on at that property than meets the eye. Otherwise, why be so secretive about it? New Yorkers are always willing to flash their money around. Who builds the biggest building in the city and doesn't plaster their name across it?"

She began to pace. "We need to do some more digging into Genesis, find out exactly who they are. It's possible they are behind the attempt on Langstrode's life."

Vida raised an eyebrow. "I thought his wife was behind it. Isn't that why you dragged her in here?"

Kasey swept her hair back behind her ear. "Yeah, I am pretty sure that his wife was behind the shooting we witnessed today, but that's not what I'm talking about. I'm talking about my vision of Langstrode being thrown off his building."

"Oh, right, I'd forgotten about that," Vida said, his eyes going wide as the realization set in. "You mean this guy has two sets of people trying to kill him?"

"It would appear that way," she replied. "In my vision, one of the men remained hidden. I only heard his voice. It's possible that he is connected to this Genesis Holdings, or at least he has the same taste for trying to conceal his identity. It's worth looking into."

Vida spun in his chair. "In my excitement about the Langstrode's I almost forgot, how did your meeting with the Arcane Council go?" Vida asked. "Follow up question, what are they like? And what did they want from you?"

"Easy with the twenty questions," she said, halting in her tracks. "Starting at the top. The meeting with the Arcane Council went about as well as I expected—it was a train wreck. The Council itself is like the Supreme Court, only older and more intimidating, because when you disobey their edicts, you wind up with your memory wiped and locked in a funny farm. They wanted to know why so much magic had been detected at the Ninth Precinct. It seems they were not aware that our Shinigami friends were in town."

"What?" Vida replied. "Aren't they meant to know when a bunch of homicidal wizards land on the East Coast?"

"You would think so," she said. "Unfortunately, it seemed to be news to them. Once I told them, rather than being concerned about a death cult bent on destroying our city, they were more interested in whether or not any normals had observed magic during the attack."

Vida licked his lips nervously. "And what did you tell them?"

"Nothing. Like I told you and Bishop, no one can know that you know my secret. Normal people will think you're crazy, and other wizards will think you're a threat. Never under any circumstances can you tell anyone what you know. Am I clear?"

He held up both hands defensively. "Crystal. So, you lied to them? Isn't that like a crime in your world?"

"Without a doubt," she said, "but it can't be any worse than the alternative. If they find out I used magic in front of the pair of you, then they will almost certainly wipe your memories, and do who knows what to me. They already warned me once, and they did it again today. If our world is discovered as a result of my actions, the punishment is likely to be death."

"Seems a little severe," he said.

"Perhaps, but you have no idea just how paranoid they can be. They consider normals to be an even bigger threat to us and our safety than other wizards, like the Shinigami. I told them about the coming attack and the fact that Cyrus was murdered. It barely seemed to even register on their radar."

"What? What were their exact words?

She shook her head. "They pretty much told me to leave it alone and let the grown-ups handle it."

Vida winced.

"And being the patient, reserved young woman you are, you agreed with their suggestion and wished them a pleasant day?" he asked, sarcasm dripping from his every syllable.

"Not exactly," she replied. "I told them I had already killed three Shinigami which is more than their collective efforts of the last century. I told them they were welcome to pitch in and help any time, but I wouldn't be leaving the city's fate in their hands."

"How did they take that?"

"Not really sure, to be honest," She said. "I stormed out of there before they could respond."

"Of course you did," he said with an exasperated sigh.

"I'm serious. We can't rely on others to save the city. I've had this vision over and over ever since I was a child. I've seen the city devastated time and time again. The ground splitting open, towering buildings shattering apart and collapsing. People screaming as their whole world comes crashing down around them. Thick green smoke choking the air. I have seen it, Vida. It's horrifying. These visions come to me for a reason. I need to do something about it. Call it fate or destiny or just dumb luck, but I've seen it coming and I can't ignore it. What if I leave it to the Council and they fail? How will I feel then?"

Vida's eyes lit up.

"What is it? Kasey asked.

Vida tapped away on his keyboard as he spoke. "Your visions, you've never mentioned the green smoke before."

"So? What's so important about the green smoke?"

"Well," Vida began as a map of New York City flashed up on the screen, "normally we would expect that the smoke from such a disaster to be grey or black from the debris. Certainly the destruction of the cityscape would result in a dust cloud in that spectrum of color.

"You may remember the footage from the World Trade Centre collapse during the 9-11 attacks. That is what we would expect to see on a wider scale. For that cloud of debris to be tinged with green, something else would have to have combined with it. If collapsing buildings didn't produce that color, then we know it has to have come from somewhere else and I think I just worked out what it is."

"I always assumed it was magic," Kasey countered.

"It could be, but it could also be Serpentinite," Vida said.

"Say what now?" Kasey asked, glancing over at him.

"Serpentinite. It's a crystalline rock formation rich in iron and magnesium. It has a distinctly green hue."

"And?" Kasey replied.

"Serpentinite is one of many layers of crystalline bedrock that runs underneath New York City. In some places, like Staten Island, it is quite near the surface. In other parts of the tri-state area, like for example underneath Manhattan, it can be found much deeper in the Earth.

"I believe that the attack you witness in your visions is a seismic event, the likes of which we have never seen here in the city. Or the United States, for that matter. If the bedrock of the city was to fracture, the subsequent pressure release would not only destroy much of the city but in the process, the Serpentinite would be ground to dust and produce the green tinged clouds you saw in your vision."

"So, you're saying these deposits of Serpentinite are beneath the city?"

"Exactly," Vida said. "Your mother mentioned that these Shinigami like to use their magic to simulate natural disasters so that they can spread fear and gather acolytes to their cause. I think they're planning to use their magic to unleash an earthquake that will level the city."

"How strong would the quake have to be to do that?" Kasey asked.

"On the Richter scale? To shatter the bedrock of the city, a ten," Vida said. "It would require immense pressure to be released in a focused burst. To put it into perspective, the earthquake that decimated Chile in 1960 was a 9.5. It was the strongest ever recorded and it caused tsunamis that killed people in Hawaii, Japan, and the Philippines. It left two million people homeless. Something that strong, in the center of New York City, could kill millions. The subsequent tidal movements would devastate the East Coast and leave millions more homeless."

Kasey's heart began to pound. Vida's description explained not only the green tinged clouds she had seen but also the tremendous motion she'd witnessed in her vision. It was the earth splitting apart beneath the city.

"That's it, Vida. That's exactly what they have planned. We have to stop them before it's too late."

"But how?" Vida turned to look at her. "I don't even understand how such an attack is even possible. How can we stop someone who wields that much power?"

Kasey shook her head. "I don't think the quake itself is fueled by magic. If it were, the Arcane Council would be able to sense it and put a stop to it. Only a fool would come here to the seat of their power and attempt a magical assault of that magnitude. It would surely alert the Council and result in swift retribution. I think they intend to set the quake in motion by more mundane means."

"What are you thinking?"

"You mentioned that stone, Serpentinite. It's buried beneath Manhattan, right?"

Vida nodded. "Yes, the most substantial deposits would be far deeper than they are in Staten Island though."

"That's why Langstrode's building is so important. You said it yourself earlier, it's one of the tallest buildings in the world and yet it has one of the smallest footprints of any in the world. One singular giant column reaching skyward. If it doesn't have a wide footprint, it would require them to dig deeper, right?"

"Much," Vida replied, nodding as he seemed to pick up on her suggestion.

"The tallest building in the city would have the deepest footing of any in the city," Kasey said, getting to her feet. "The construction is a cover-up. They're going to use it to destroy the city."

CHAPTER 12

Martin Langstrode struggled to sleep, tossing and turning on the borrowed sofa. The makeshift bed belonged to Alicia's boyfriend, Dante, and it was a good six inches shorter than Martin needed it to be.

While sofa was uncomfortable, it wasn't the sofa that was keeping him awake. It was the knowledge that in spite of everything that had happened, he knew he still had to go home.

The small supply of drugs he had was stashed in his room at home. Without retrieving and selling them, he didn't stand a chance of gathering the money he needed to repay Lester. The last thing he wanted was to endure another beating.

As the night wore on, Martin grew more restless. Giving up on sleep, he headed into the kitchen and found himself a beer in the fridge. He had drained almost half the bottle when he realized he wasn't alone. Turning, he saw Dante standing in the doorway.

Martin raised the bottle. "Hey, sorry about the beer. I would have asked but I didn't think anyone was still up."

"Don't worry about it," Dante replied with a smile.

Something about Dante's grin rubbed Martin the wrong way.

Dante must have sensed his uneasiness. "What's got you bothered?"

"It's a long story," Martin replied, then downed another long draught of the beer.

Dante folded his arms. "Got anything to do with that beating you took?" "What beating?" Martin leaned against the bench, trying to play it cool.

"What beating?" Dante laughed. "My friend, that bruise under your eye is still visible, when you walked in you were limping, and if I had to guess, I'd say the shallow breaths are a result of someone dancing on your ribs. How am I doing?"

"How did you guess?" Martin answered.

Dante strode to the fridge and took out a beer for himself. "I've had a few in my day. Who did it? Loan shark, dealer, or someone who just didn't take a liking to you?"

"What makes you think it might be a loan shark or a dealer?"

"If it wasn't, I'm sure an East Sider like yourself would have gone straight to the police. You wouldn't be crashed here on my couch if it was a mugging gone wrong. Nope, you owe someone money and that's their way of reminding you that they are serious about collecting. How much are you in the hole for?"

"Twenty grand," Martin answered with a sigh.

"Youch, wish I could help," Dante answered. "I don't have that kind of cash."

"No, man, don't worry about it. It's my problem. I'll deal with it. You are doing enough already. Besides, I have a plan. I just need to get home and collect a few things. If I can avoid my murderous mother, I should be able to get what I need to raise some funds."

"You're heading back there? From what your sister was saying, your mom might be armed. Are you sure that's wise?"

Martin drained the dregs of his beer. "I don't know about wise, but it's my only play. Mom might kill me, but my loan shark definitely will if I don't make him whole."

"Take your gun. Just in case," Dante suggested. "Better to have it and not need it, then need it and not have it."

"A gun, are you kidding? I don't have a gun," Martin protested.

"Hmmm." Dante strode to the cupboard. Reaching for the top shelf, he lifted down a small box and placed it on the counter. He lifted the lid off the tin, then drew out a compact black pistol with a brown grip.

He held out the pistol to Martin.

"I can't take that," Martin said. "I have a record. If I get caught carrying a weapon..." he trailed off as Dante burst into laughter.

"If you are caught without it, you may wind up dead. It sounds like your mom is willing to do whatever it takes. At least have something you can defend yourself with if you need to. The serial number has been filed off so it's completely untraceable. If you get in trouble, toss it in the river."

Martin gingerly took the pistol. It was heavier than he had expected. It had been years since he had last held a gun.

"Have you ever fired a pistol before?" Dante asked.

"It's been a while," Martin admitted. "Dad and I used to go to the range when I was younger. It's been years though."

"Well, it's just like riding a bike. Don't even worry about it. Someone gets in your face, then you simply point-and-shoot. Make sure that there isn't anything important between you and what you want to hit. It's not much, but it will keep you safe. Just keep it concealed unless you need to use it."

"I don't know how to thank you," Martin said.

"I do," Dante answered. "There are some things that your sister needs for class. With your mom on her killing spree, I won't let her go near the place, but your sister can't go without them forever. I need you to grab her laptop and some other bits and pieces. Can you do that?"

"Yeah, I guess so," Martin said.

Dante rested his hand on Martin's shoulder. "Look, Martin, there is no need to worry. If what Alicia has told me is true, you've already been written out of the will, so you're not really a threat to your mother and she has no reason to hurt you. On the other hand, Alicia can contest the estate. If Sal writes your mother out of the will, Alicia will be target number one. I've gotta keep her safe, and I can't do that if she is running back to the apartment to get the things she needs. I want you to get them for me."

"Just get me a list," Martin replied. "I'll take care of the rest."

Dante reached into his pocket and drew out a slip of paper. "Here it is. Take her duffel as well. It's over by the front door. You'll need something to carry everything back. It has a lot of her old textbooks in it. Could you swap those with the ones by the laptop?"

"Why don't we just leave those here?" Martin asked. "It'd be a lot easier."

"You know your sister. She's a neat freak. Doesn't want to leave stuff all over the place. She's worried she'll lose it. Anyway, your mom can't keep this up forever. Sooner or later, she'll be in jail and you'll both be able to return home. Alicia wants her stuff there when she gets back. Can you do that, Martin?"

"Of course," Martin replied. After all, this was the most kindness anyone had shown him in weeks. Picking up few of his sister's things was a small price to pay for a safe place to crash. Not to mention the weapon.

It might come in handy. Not just for the trip to his home, but if Lester wanted to give him another beating, it might make him think twice.

Martin thought better of it.

Lester is crazy. If I pulled a gun on him, I'd have to shoot him. Anything else would result in him beating me to death.

"Thanks, Martin. I'm going to head up to bed. Stay safe. I'll see you tomorrow." Dante dropped his empty bottle in the trash and disappeared down the hallway, leaving Martin alone with his thoughts.

The rest of the night rolled past slowly. As the sun rose, Martin abandoned any hope of sleep. Rising from the couch, he tucked the pistol into his trousers and headed for the front door. He grabbed his backpack from the chair and slung it over his shoulder. As he made his way out the front door, he spotted the duffel bag and remembered his promise to Dante.

Grabbing the duffel bag, he hoisted it onto his other shoulder.

Geez, sis. Who uses this many textbooks?

Martin sighed and slipped out the front door.

The sun gradually rose over the East River, but New York City was already awake. Pedestrians thronged the street, some in suits heading to work, others in their sportswear running toward Central Park.

This is too early to be awake.

The brisk walk he was currently taking across the city would normally be considered unthinkable before 7am. The benefits of being a Langstrode had allowed him some luxuries and latitude in life. More than a few, if he was being honest with himself.

He had never needed to hold down a real job. Instead, he had interned at his father's company until the relationship had soured. After his recent arrest, the work environment had become somewhat hostile.

Martin paused at the edge of the sidewalk as the light above flashed red. Other pedestrians continued crossing but Martin had seen enough cyclists and pedestrians killed by impatient drivers that he wasn't willing to risk it. He was in enough pain already. His ribs were still tender but the swelling in his face had gone down considerably.

He had almost considered asking his father for the money to pay Lester. After all, it would only be chump change to his father. Back when his parents had furnished him with a credit card he could max out each month, life had been easy. He'd lived comfortably in the knowledge that the balance would be settled by his parents. Unfortunately, those days were gone. He'd bounced from one job to another as his habits continued to take their toll.

Lester had been his dealer, and Martin his prize customer. Now, Martin had nothing to pay with and had been forced to deal instead. After all, Lester recognized Martin still had a group of wealthy Upper East Side friends who loved to party. It was far from ideal, but he was making enough cash to get by.

The peace was short lived, though. When Martin had tried to deal to an undercover cop, he'd been arrested and his backpack full of product had been seized as evidence. Now he owed Lester a small fortune, and he'd been written out of his father's will. Not that it mattered; at his current rate it seemed likely he would not survive his father. At least he had thought so until all hell broke loose yesterday.

Alicia had called the night before, warning him not to go home. According to his sister and the police, Mother had hired someone to try and gun down their father.

That's just typical. She wants everything to herself.

With Martin written out of the will and Alicia still under twenty-five, there would be no one to contest the estate. Alicia's inheritance would be placed in a trust administered by their mother, who would double as executor for his father's estate. Martin doubted that status quo would exist for much longer, but he couldn't help but be shocked by their temerity of his mother.

Alicia's call had come just in time and fortunately, she had been willing to let Martin crash with her, or more accurately, her boyfriend Dante, for the night. The couch was no penthouse, but it was better than the alternative.

Dante had not been at all what Martin had expected. Alicia was only twenty-one; Dante was easily thirty but seemed to be doing alright. He owned a Harley, which led Martin to believe that perhaps their parents didn't know as much about Dante as he may have thought.

As Martin made his way down Fifth Avenue, he thought about his current course of action. He could feel the Colt tucked into his trousers. The cool steel was a comfort to him as he bore down on the luxury apartments he had called home for most of his life.

When he reached the building, the doorman, Chauncy, waved. It was difficult to picture that in this spot less than a day ago, his father had almost been gunned down by a hit man.

Martin nodded to Chauncey as he passed by.

He strode across the lobby. Its rich decor of polished porcelain tiles had been freshly mopped by the morning janitorial crew. From the door to the bank of elevators, a plush red-carpet runner crossed the lobby. The runner seemed to be styled after the red carpets of Hollywood. Martin couldn't help but admire the genius in the interior decorator's choice. The lavish room was furnished so as to coddle the sensation of self-importance that the Upper East Siders felt. It was the very sensation that kept them paying thousands and, in some instances, tens of thousands of dollars, in rent each and every week.

Martin reached the bank of elevators. The exterior doors were finished in gold leaf, not the usual drab aluminum one would expect. He pressed the call button, then paced back and forth as he waited for the elevator.

"Is everything alright, sir?" a voice called from the lobby.

Martin glanced behind him to find Nigel, the building manager, watching him with interest. The silver-haired steward's smile melted into a frown at the sight of Martin. He shrugged it off. He was used to Nigel's disdain.

Nigel's gaze was locked on Martin and the duffel he was carrying. It was clear from the disdainful expression he always wore that Nigel only tolerated Martin on account of his family. The Langstrodes paid a small fortune for their penthouse and though Nigel might loathe him, there was little he could do while Martin still enjoyed his father's protection.

"Perfectly fine, Nigel. No need to trouble yourself here," Martin replied

Nigel's gaze wandered from Martin's eyes to the bag and back.

Fortunately, the elevator doors parted. Martin stepped onto the lift.

"Would you like a hand with your bags, sir?" Nigel called as he headed toward him. "I can ride with you."

"No need," Martin replied, mashing the buttons to close the door.

The gilded doors closed before Nigel could make it down the hallway. The elevator sped upward. Martin watched the LED display gradually move from left to right above the door, all the while contemplating what he might do if he saw his mother. He was placing a lot of stock in what Dante had said. He was no longer a threat, so why would she try to harm him?

As he approached the penthouse, Martin's confidence began to waver. He wanted to believe that she wouldn't kill anyone, but if she was willing to hire a hit man, then pulling the trigger herself wasn't too great a leap.

With one hand, Martin reached behind his back, ensuring the pistol was still wedged firmly in his jeans. As his hand brushed the cold steel, he breathed out. The Colt had been a mainstay of the military for decades. It may have only carried seven rounds, but its stopping power had been felt in each war the US had fought in the past four decades.

Classical music lilted from a speaker by the buttons, but the notes did nothing to soothe Martin's nerves. He'd always been more into jazz than the classics.

Martin's stomach flipped as the elevator came to a halt. The doors parted, and Martin stepped out onto the familiar landing. There was only one door, and it led straight to his penthouse.

My home.

It certainly didn't feel that way now, though.

Martin took out his phone and dialed his sister. After three rings, she answered.

"Martin, what's up?"

"I've just stopped by home to grab some things. I thought I'd give you a call, just in case anything happens. If mom's home and she flips out, at least someone will know where I was."

"Good idea," Alicia said. "I don't think it was a great idea to go home, though. Who knows what she is capable of right now."

Martin approached the door. With the phone still squished to his left ear, he pressed his right ear up against the door. He couldn't hear anything. There was no movement coming from the penthouse.

"Are you there, Martin?" Alicia asked.

"I am. I'm just trying to see if I can hear anything. I don't know that anyone is home."

"That's good, isn't it?" Alicia answered. "Get in and get out quickly, before she comes back."

Martin set the duffel down and patted his pockets. He had to change hands with the phone, so he could reach into his back-left pocket. Pulling out his key, he slid it into the lock. With a gentle turn, the door opened.

Martin slid the key back into his pocket, took the phone with his left hand, picked up the duffel bag, and entered the apartment.

Martin tiptoed across the lounge and into the hall that led to his room. Reaching for the gold doorknob, he twisted it and the door opened.

His room was just as he had left it. There was some dirty washing laying scattered about the floor. The bed was still unmade and the glass sliding doors that led to the balcony were open. Only the security screen was shut. It allowed a breeze to blow in from outside.

"Martin, what are you up to?" Alicia asked through the phone.

"I'm just grabbing some things from my room. Give me a minute and then I will grab the stuff for you. It's all in your room, right?"

"It should be. It's pretty tidy, so it shouldn't be too hard find."

"Alright, just a minute."

He sat the phone down next to him as he lay on the carpet. Pushing forward, he slid his head to the edge of the bed, then reached his arms underneath. After a moment, he found the incision he'd made in the bottom of his mattress. The slip allowed him to store his stash somewhere the maids would never stumble across. Reaching inside the slip, he drew out three small packages and a small roll of cash. With the slip emptied, he slid out from under the edge of the bed. As he did so, his attention was drawn to the door where a figure was standing. It was his mother.

"I should have known you'd come back for your drugs," she chided. "I raised you better."

"Yes, sage advice from a would-be murderer," Martin replied as he sat up and drew the Colt, pointing it directly at his mother. "I'm just grabbing a few things and then I'm leaving. Stay out of my way. No one needs to get hurt."

Her eyes bulged at the sight of the weapon. "Martin what are you doing? Why have you got a gun? Don't point that thing at me."

His heart pounded in his chest. "I figured it would be helpful to be able to defend myself. After all, you did try to kill Dad yesterday."

"I did not. That was Leith. Even the police agree. That's why I'm here and he's still in custody."

Martin shook his head. "I don't want to hear the lies, alright? I'll only be here for a few minutes, so stay out of my way, okay?"

A bead of sweat ran down his brow.

There was a muffled noise from his phone beside him. He'd forgot all about it.

He grabbed the phone and pressed it to his ear. It was Alicia.

"Martin, what's going on?" Alicia demanded.

Cynthia's face turned red, "Who's on the phone Martin?"

Martin ignored his mother, preferring to speak to Alicia. "It's Mom. She's here. She showed up when I was in my room. She must have been sleeping or something."

There was a pause and silence at the other end of the phone.

"Alicia, can you hear me? She's here. Stay on the line. If anything happens, call the police." He turned to his mother. "Did you hear that? The phone is live. You try anything, and she'll go straight to the police."

Cynthia held up both hands defensively. "I'm not going to kill my own son. We've had our problems, but I'm not a monster."

Martin set the phone back down as he began to gather his things off the floor. "I'm sure you never thought you'd try to kill your own husband, either. Until you decided there wasn't enough money to go around. Good thing the cops showed up before your little friend could finish the job."

He opened the duffel to tuck his stash inside. The duffel was loaded with dirty laundry and a few textbooks.

No wonder it's so dang heavy.

"It wasn't me, Martin, I swear. The call came from Leith's phone. He called the hit on your dad. Obviously, he got a taste of the high life and wanted to move in. I never would have allowed it. Your father and I may have been unhappy, but I'm not a murderer."

He pulled out the textbooks and dirty laundry so that he could pack his stash into the duffel.

As he did so, a glimmer of red caught his eye. He burrowed into the duffel and found it. It was thin and cylindrical.

A wire.

Martin hastily removed the other contents from the bag. The red wire ran to a small parcel. It looked like a small brick wrapped in brown paper. There was something printed on it but from where he was, he couldn't read it. Taped to the front of the brick was a cell phone. The red wire was one of a series of wires running between the phone and the small brick.

His heart stopped.

It's a bomb.

"How the hell did that get in there?" Martin demanded, as he picked up the bag and looked for somewhere to get rid of the bomb.

"What is it?" Cynthia asked.

"There's a bomb in the bag."

She froze where she was. "Get rid of it."

His gaze settled on the door to the balcony. He had no idea how much devastation the bomb might unleash, but if he didn't do something quick, he was a dead man.

He took a step toward the door but stopped.

A faint ringing rose from the duffel. Martin looked inside to see the phone flashing.

Oh...

The bomb detonated. Martin's eyes blinked at the sudden blaze of light before the blast tore both the duffel and him apart in an instant.

CHAPTER 13

Manhattan's Upper East side was in complete disarray. At Bishop's suggestion, Kasey had taken the subway. She emerged from the station to find traffic gridlock all around her.

It was her second visit to the luxury apartments in as many days. Yesterday it had been an active shooter. Today an explosion had rocked the neighborhood.

Stretching for blocks in every direction, angry commuters fumed as police and emergency services tried to direct traffic.

Kasey had been on her way into the station when she had received the call from Bishop. It had been clipped and brief as was her style, but Kasey struggled to believe it.

A bomb had detonated in the Upper East Side. It was difficult to believe, harder still to picture.

She made her way down the sidewalk toward the prestigious Fifth Avenue apartments, pressing through the throng of people that were peering skyward. As she reached the building, she hit the police cordon. A row of officers stood shoulder to shoulder to try and keep the curious pedestrians back. The road was entirely blocked with squad cars, fire trucks, and ambulances.

Kasey stepped into the street to slip around the cordon but was stopped by an officer she didn't recognize.

"Hold it there, miss. The whole area has been sealed off. It's not safe for you to proceed. You'll have to find another way around."

Kasey pulled her ID from her pocket and flashed it to the officer. "I'm with the Ninth Precinct. That entire scene is part of our ongoing investigation. My detective is already on site, and she asked me to come over."

"Just a moment. I'll ring it in." The officer stepped away and clutched his radio. Pressing down on the transmit button, he began. "This is Officer Thompson at the southern cordon. I have a young woman here. She says she is with the Ninth Precinct, claims her detective is on site. Please advise."

There was a crackle of static and the radio burst to life.

"Officer Thompson, this is Bishop from the Ninth Precinct. She is one of our technicians. Send her through, please."

"Understood, Bishop. Sending her in now." The officer stepped back to the barrier and waved Kasey through. "You are free to head in. Be careful, there is debris everywhere. You'll need to tread carefully."

"Thanks," Kasey replied as she stepped past the cordon.

She picked up the pace as she headed up Fifth Avenue. With each step she took toward the Langstrode's apartment, the more the gravity of what had occurred sank in.

Shattered glass blanketed the street ahead of her. Sheets of drywall and plasterboard were strewn everywhere. As she walked toward the Langstrode's luxury apartment, the devastation only intensified. A twisted steel girder had landed on top of a taxicab, crushing its roof in.

She hoped that no one had been in the car at the time but judging from its position in the center of the street, she found that unlikely. First responders were clearing the debris from the street, but based on what Kasey could see, there was hours, perhaps days of work ahead of them.

As Kasey scanned Central Park to her left, she saw what looked like a ceiling fan that had been blown clear of the building, embedded in the green grass of the park.

Crossing the street, she finally got her first look at the Langstrode's building.

She stopped dead, her racing heart skipping a beat. The entire top of the luxury apartments had been blown to smithereens. What should have been the top three floors and the Langstrode's penthouse was now a smoldering wreckage. It looked like a creature from a Hollywood movie had torn the top off the building. Jagged mounts and internal reinforcement lay exposed, and much of the glass for several floors beneath had also been blown out. The Langstrode's apartment was entirely gone. Just gone. The better part of two floors beneath it had been severely damaged. Smoke rose into the air, a steady plume of wispy black mist that ascended until it blended with the storm clouds overhead.

What the hell?

"Kasey, over here," Bishop shouted. "Let's go!"

Kasey followed the voice toward the front door of the building and spotted Bishop beckoning to her.

Kasey blinked as she fought to clear her mind. The shock of the sight of the devastated building was clouding her mind. It was difficult to imagine she had been inside it only hours ago. Now the Langstrode's apartment and anyone in it was gone forever.

"What happened here?" Kasey asked.

"We're still piecing that together. An hour ago, a bomb exploded in the penthouse. From what we've been able to gather from the areas of the building we do have access to, the penthouse has been wiped out. So have most of the two floors below it. Below that, there is further structural damage, not enough to bring down the building but we have evacuated it. From the top three floors, we've been unable to locate twelve residents, including Mrs. Langstrode, who was in the building at the time."

Kasey raised an eyebrow, "Cynthia is dead? Well, well, well. Seems karma is awfully quick these days."

"Kasey!" Bishop chastised. "The woman's dead."

"Yeah, that banshee was a murderer and a sly one at that. The city is not gonna miss her."

Bishop's face was drawn but when Kasey looked closer, Bishop's puffy red eyes were visible. The detective had been crying.

"The city may not miss her, but there are other innocent people that were hurt here. Spare a thought for them before you make a joke."

Kasey remembered the cab she had passed by. It was true. Many innocent victims had been caught up in the devastation.

"I'm sorry, Bishop. I shouldn't have." Changing the topic, she looked up and said, "What are we looking at? How many have been injured?"

"As I said, we still have over a dozen missing residents. Several others have been confirmed dead already. Debris related trauma from the explosion has done further damage. We have four dead bystanders who were simply on the street below when the blast went off. Another fifteen have been injured by falling debris or traffic accidents that occurred after the blast."

Kasey shook her head. "Do we know what caused it?"

"Definitely a bomb," Bishop replied. "The bomb squad is still picking their way through the upper floors. Based on their early analysis, they believe it was an improvised explosive device. Likely C4. The building supervisor says that Martin Langstrode entered the building minutes before the blast. The supervisor said he was acting suspicious and carrying a large black duffel. It's possible the bomb was Martin's retaliation against his mother."

"A bomb seems out of character. Why not just shoot her?"

"No idea. We'll ask him when we find him."

"You think he survived?" Kasey asked.

"We aren't sure," Bishop replied, "but you've met the kid. Suicide bomber doesn't really seem like his M.O. Martin has lived here for years. It's possible he dropped the duffel and made it out of the hotel amid the chaos after it went off. We are still trying to get access to surveillance footage from the building, but much of its systems are still down. Nearby surveillance cameras haven't picked up anything yet but there's still dozens of buildings to canvas."

Kasey looked at the devastation around her. "It's hard to believe the kid has this in him, though. Dealing drugs is one thing, but blowing up a building, that is a big leap from his previous record."

"We can ask him about it once we have him in custody," Bishop said. "I'm sure a stint at Rikers is going to be a lifestyle adjustment after living in this palace all his life."

Kasey stared up at the luxury apartments, taking in the shattered surface of the building and the smoke billowing out from its roof.

"How are you sure he even got out?" Kasey asked. "If the supervisor said he entered only minutes before, there is a chance he never made it out. He may have been in the penthouse when it blew."

Bishop nodded. "There's always a chance. Right now, the evidence from the penthouse is strewn over three city blocks and part of Central Park. We will be gathering evidence and combing through wreckage for days. We have no way of knowing if he got out or not, until we find some trace of him in the apartment, or on the streets below."

Kasey fought back the urge to vomit. She normally had a pretty strong stomach but the thought of a body being spread over three city blocks was enough to make her queasy.

"In any event, we have to be careful," Bishop said. "If he did survive the blast, we need to pick him up quickly, before he tries to leave the city, or worse yet, sets off any other bombs."

"You think he'll run?" Kasey asked tucking her wayward hair back behind her ear.

"Hard to tell," Bishop responded. "We would have never predicted this after our meeting with him. But if he's willing to blow up his mother, there's a decent chance he'll go after that loan shark that gave him the beating. We need to be on the lookout. He'll have every government department in the country after him, I doubt he'll get far. My main worry is what he does between now and when we catch him."

"Unless of course he was in there." Kasey nodded at the building. "Then we can be sure he isn't going to be up to a whole lot of anything anymore."

Bishop nodded. "That's why I wanted you down here. I was kind of hoping you'd be able to help us narrow down our leads.

"So, we're heading up?" Kasey asked.

Bishop rested her hands on her hips. "I wish we could, but the place is still in lock-down. Our protocols are severe. No one else can go into the building until it's been swept for other explosives. The bomb squad are still going floor by floor. It will be a while before they're finished."

"Then why come down here if we can't get into the site?" Kasey asked. "Wouldn't we be better off chasing down leads somewhere else?"

"What leads, Kasey? The woman that tried to gun down her husband yesterday is now dead. Her apartment is in smoking ruin. As far as Sal Langstrode goes, he's probably safer than he was yesterday. Unfortunately for us, we now have a mass murder and homicide case on our hands, and we aren't even certain who is responsible. I was hoping your being here might spark some inspiration." Bishop awkwardly winked at Kasey, the left side of her face screwing up as she tried to keep one eye open.

"Was that a wink, Bishop? Because if it was, it was awful," Kasey teased.

"Gah, you said we had to keep your" —Bishop's voice dropped to a whisper— "powers on the down low. I was trying to be subtle."

Kasey laughed, "We're going to have to practice that. Besides, they don't work like that. I have to be closer to the victim or the scene. As it is, that apartment is more than fifteen stories above us. I'm not gonna get anything from down here. I've gotta get closer."

Bishop looked at the entrance of the building. "Not gonna happen. The bomb destroyed the elevators and the staircases are full of bomb squad officers sweeping the building. They will not react well to anyone else being inside. Even us, no matter how good our excuse is."

Kasey could see that Bishop wasn't going to budge. "Okay, I'll take a walk round the block and see if I can't pick something up, but I'm warning you. Don't get your hopes up. There is no guarantee I'll have a vision."

"That's all we can ask, Kasey. Give it your best shot. I'm going to canvass the nearby buildings, make sure we get any surveillance footage of the area before and after the blast. If Martin did get out, he has to have been picked up on a camera somewhere."

With a nod, Bishop turned and headed down East Hundred and Second Street, leaving Kasey to consider the devastation before her.

She decided to set out in the other direction. If she could circle the building, perhaps she might find something that would trigger a vision. Any insight into the bombing would help. From what Bishop had said, she seemed to think that the threat to Sal Langstrode had been dealt with. Bishop was confident that his wife Cynthia had ordered the hit. With the hitman dead and Cynthia sharing his fate, even Kasey had to agree that on the surface it seemed like Sal might be safe.

As she made her way around the luxury apartments, she thought about the vision she had seen when she first met Langstrode. He had been standing on the unfinished floor of the sky rise. Her visions had never failed to eventuate before. She wondered what part her interference might have had on the Sal's fate.

By thwarting Cynthia's plot, have we set in motion a series of events that will culminate in Sal being thrown to his death?

Or was that a plot that had always been in motion? Simply waiting for the day, for the opportune moment to strike.

She had so many questions about her gift. Questions that there was simply no answer to. Prescience was not common, even among witches. Most of the books written on the subject were the writings of charlatans. Truly prescient witches and wizards were extremely rare. Kasey had sought them out in her youth but never succeeded in finding a truly gifted individual.

Even among witches and wizards the prescient were shunned. People always said that they wanted to know what the future held, but people were liars. They only wanted to know what was coming if it was positive, if it was a tragedy or misfortune, they tended to lash out, blaming the messenger rather than themselves for what their future held.

As a witch, she was inexperienced and as a prescient, she was infantile. She was only able to see that which her gift forced upon her. Many times, she had tried patiently to summon a glimpse of the future only to waste hours of her time in meditation.

Instead, she was forced to rely on catalysts—victims of violent crimes or other extremes of emotion—to act as triggers for her visions.

She rounded the corner and headed up the side of the building, gingerly stepping over a steel beam that had twisted free of the structure. Glass was everywhere.

The explosion appeared to have shattered several windows on the neighboring building also.

That blast must have been massive. If Martin had made the bomb, he'd certainly had help. There was no way an amateur could have constructed such an effective device.

Then again, the Internet is loaded with all the wrong kinds of information and plenty of people looking to cause chaos.

Kasey made a mental note to look into the Langstrode's browser history. Perhaps they might find an accomplice or at least someone responsible for giving Martin the knowledge he needed to blow up the building.

She was working her way along the glass-strewn alleyway when her phone rang. Reaching inside her jacket pocket, she lifted it out. Caller ID identified the caller as Vida.

She took the call and raised the phone to her ear. "Vida, what's up? I'm just on site with Bishop."

"I heard. A bombing, that's insane. What's going on there?"

She glanced around. "Half of the upper east side is closed off. There are first responders everywhere. The bomb squad is still scouring the building searching for any other explosives, so we can't get in. I've never seen anything like it, Vida. The top of the building is just gone, the entire floor peeled apart from the inside out. You should be glad our morgue is off-line, because whatever is left of these victims, it's scattered over three city blocks. It would be the most macabre jigsaw puzzle you've ever seen."

Vida sighed. "Oh, that's a pity. I've always loved jigsaw puzzles."

"That's just typical," Kasey said. "You're always complaining about how much work you have. Now you get a week off while the morgue is rebuilt, and you are complaining that you are missing out on the action."

"Well, not all the action, Kasey. I've been pretty busy here."

Vida's tone gave Kasey hope. She could almost feel his smug smile through the phone.

"Did you find something?" she asked.

"Oh, you could say that," Vida said. "I found Langstrode's mysterious benefactor. I know who his partner is."

CHAPTER 14

K asey stopped dead. She had been eager for any sign of who might be after Langstrode. While it seemed like every member of his family wanted him dead, Kasey doubted that their familial warfare held any bearing on the attack on New York City.

She was far more interested in who Langstrode's mysterious benefactor was. Who had appeared from nowhere looking to build the monstrosity at Park Avenue?

By his own admission, the building wasn't Langstrode's idea. He was simply a minion in the master plot. It was whoever wanted the building construction to proceed that Kasey was interested in.

Vida's insight was just what she had been looking for. After all, Langstrode had been unwilling to disclose his benefactor. There had to be a reason why.

Kasey realized she'd gone silent.

"Well, what are you waiting for, Vida? Tell me who it is."

"Oh Kasey," Vida began, "you're never going to believe this."

"After seeing the top blown off a building, the ceiling on what I believe is possible is growing by the moment. Tell me what you found."

"It's the Ainsleys, Kasey. Arthur Ainsley is Langstrode's business partner."

"What?" Kasey demanded abruptly.

"It's true!" Vida answered. "I had the devil's job trying to uncover the trail. They certainly went to great efforts to conceal it, but I can tell you that the Ainsleys are involved. No doubt about it."

"Tell me everything. What makes you so sure it's them?" Kasey asked.

"Well, I did a search to try and determine who was behind the current project with Langstrode. All I could find was a private LLC by the name of Genesis Holdings. I dug into their history, but it was a relatively new company. Simply a shell to hold the land while it is being redeveloped. Its director was a man whose name I've never seen before. I had the station do a search on him, but he came up clean. I dug a little deeper and discovered he is a floating CEO, a man organizations use when they want to remain anonymous. They are simply renting his name and identity to use for the company."

"How did you get from him to Arthur Ainsley?" Kasey asked, biting her lip nervously.

"Well, I figured if the LLC was only a few years old, then the land title had to be transferred. I went down to the title transfer office to search for the record and what would you know? They were missing. I found that little coincidence to be just a little convenient, so I kept thinking. Someone was clearly trying to cover the trail, but I managed to find an older title transfer. It was almost a decade old and related to when the apartment buildings were originally purchased. There was a copy of the contract on record and when I saw the purchaser's solicitor, I knew I was on the right track."

"What makes you say that?" Kasey asked

"Because the solicitors were Hitchcock and Maine. Names that I'd seen before. It took me a little while to work out where I'd seen them and then it clicked. That was the firm that served you with John Ainsley's lawsuit. As I dug further into the company that had acquired the property, I become suspicious. I searched through the city's applications for redevelopment, and there was one lodged almost fifteen years ago, right before the property was transferred. It was a joint application between one Asher Nasoon and Arthur Ainsley. He signed it himself. Lodged by the same firm, Hitchcock and Maine. The city rejected the application but that didn't stop them. I'm positive Ainsley then purchased the building."

"Why would he purchase it after he was knocked back for redevelopment?" Kasey asked.

"I looked through the purchase contracts," Vida replied. "After the application to redevelop was turned down by the city, the value of the land plummeted. Older buildings require far more maintenance. As it plummeted, the bank sought additional security for its existing loan and when Nasoon couldn't refinance the property, it was sold for a fraction of its former value. While we can't be certain that it was Ainsley, we know that the purchaser's solicitor was Hitchcock and Maine—Ainsley's solicitors."

Kasey punched the air jubilantly. "So, he screwed the development application on purpose to acquire property for a steal?" Kasey asked.

"Exactly," Vida said. "Doubtless he used some of his friends at City Hall to ensure it went through smoothly. The current application to redevelop 432 Park Avenue was approved in record time. Eighteen days from the date of filing to the date of the application being granted. If that's not wheels being greased, I don't know what is. That kind of influence takes money. Ainsley money."

Kasey headed for the street. She needed to find Bishop. "Thanks, Vida. That's great work."

"What are you going to do?"

"I don't know yet. I still have to figure that out. Arthur Ainsley and I aren't exactly on speaking terms after my outburst at the Arcane Council."

"Well, whatever you do, be careful. However irritating John may have been, Arthur Ainsley is another beast altogether. He's been wielding political influence in this city for more than four decades. We are going to need a lot more evidence to even think about taking him on."

"You have no idea. Arthur Ainsley is also the head of the Arcane Council. So, while he might have considerable political influence in your world, he owns mine. He has the full backing of our law enforcement community at his disposal. I need to talk to Bishop. You take care and don't tell anyone what you just told me."

"Understood. Remember, make sure you don't do anything foolish."

"No promises," Kasey replied, then hung up the phone.

She clenched her fists as she remembered the dressing down she had received in front of the Arcane Council. Of course Arthur wanted her to leave it alone. It seemed Ainsley was up to his eyeballs in whatever was going on at Park Avenue.

Could Ainsley be behind the attempt on Langstrode's life? Was it all a ploy to intimidate his new partner? Was it to force his hand, or was he angling to purchase the development from Sal's estate?

Kasey wanted to speak to Langstrode. Now that she knew who his benefactor was, she was positive she could leverage more information out of him.

What will I do about Arthur, though?

Arthur had already made it abundantly clear that he had no issues using the weight of his office to crush anyone who got in his way. She needed a plan and she needed help. She took great comfort at having Vida and Bishop on her side, but she needed more help than they could give her right now.

It was nice to have someone to speak to, but there was so much about the World of Magic they simply didn't know or didn't understand. When she had faced Danilo, she'd been alone. It had worn her down, mentally and physically. At least with their help Kasey didn't feel alone.

I need to talk to my mother. She understands far more about council politics than I do. Perhaps she will have an idea.

"There you are," Bishop said, heading toward her. "What are you doing hiding out down here, Kasey? Did you find something?"

"No visions yet, if that's what you're asking. But I did get a call from Vida. He's tracked down Langstrode's partner. You'll never guess who it is."

"Forgive me, Kasey, I'm not really in a mood for guessing games," Bishop replied.

"It's Arthur Ainsley. He bought the land after tanking the previous owner's development application with the City Council. He's the one who hired Langstrode for the development. Somehow, he's got a hand in all of this."

"Ainsley?" Bishop shook her head. "You've got to be kidding me. It was bad enough when his son was coming after you. Arthur is an animal. Taking him down, it just can't be done. We don't have enough clout."

"Well, we're going to have to get some," Kasey replied, wringing her hands. "If Arthur is behind the development and the development has something to do with the attack on New York City, we need to stop them before it's too late."

"That's the problem, Kasey. To stop Ainsley, we'll need to catch him red handed. We need to see him pulling the trigger or breaking the law. Unless we have that, we may as well not bother. He has enough lawyers and political influence, he'll be back on the streets in minutes. We can't afford to go after him half-hearted."

Kasey nodded. "What we need is a plan."

"Yeah, we do, but now is not the time. We have a lead on Martin Langstrode. Apparently, his credit card was used to hire a storage unit in Queens. We're going to check it out, see what he was doing there."

"Now?" Kasey asked. "What about Ainsley?"

"Ainsley is going to have to wait. Martin just blew up an apartment building. He's at the top of our hit list. We've got to get to him before he can do any more damage. One of the bomb squad units are coming with us. We need to ensure there are no explosive at the storage unit. We're rolling out now." Bishop pointed to the street.

Kasey followed her out to the squad car, opened the door, and slid into the passenger seat. As soon as the door shut, Bishop turned the key and the car roared to life. Flicking on the lights, she waited while nearby officers parted the roadblock. The traffic heading south on Fifth Avenue had been cut off entirely, leaving Bishop and Kasey with a relatively clear run to East 59th Street. The bomb squad's jet black armored car lumbered along behind, with two other squad cars bringing up the rear.

Bishop made the turn onto East 59th Street and was met with New York City traffic at its finest.

"We don't have time for this," Bishop stated, flicking on the sirens.

The squad car's sirens blared to life, startling nearby pedestrians and drivers alike. Slowly but surely, the traffic ahead parted to allow the police procession to pass.

The squad car hurtled along East 59th Street and then up onto the Queensboro Bridge. Kasey glanced out the window at the East River as it came and went. Roosevelt Island too passed in moments and soon Bishop was on the east bank heading into Astoria.

Pedestrians stared at the convoy as it made its way through the suburb.

As traffic eased, Bishop killed the sirens.

"I can't tell you how much I hate those," Kasey replied. "Any loud repetitive noise drives me nuts. But it's like whoever designed that siren scientifically formulated it to agitate me."

"That's the point. If it's annoying enough, people will want to get out of the way. They will do just about anything to get it to pass by. We might have been stuck in that traffic for a half-hour. And that's time that we just don't have to waste."

Kasey nodded. "So, what's the plan?"

"Well, in light of the bombing at the apartments, we're going have to clear the storage area. Once we have established a perimeter and know that the facility is empty, the bomb squad will enter and ensure that it isn't a trap. They will sweep for any further explosive devices and then we will search for evidence. If Martin was willing to blow up his own mother, there's no telling what else he might do."

"You think he'll go after other targets?" Kasey asked.

"I wouldn't want to be Lester Colton," Bishop replied. "He would have to be pretty high on any hit list. Martin has already shown a disregard for collateral damage. We have to scoop him up before he can set off another bomb."

Bishop slowed down as the squad car reached the self-storage facility. Hundreds of storage sheds stretched into the distance. Bishop pulled into the parking lot and killed the engine, but she left the lights going. Black Betty, the bomb squad's heavy armored truck, rolled in behind her. The remaining squad cars blocked the driveway to ensure no one else could enter.

Bishop and Kasey climbed out of the car. Kasey grabbed her crime scene kit off the back seat and followed Bishop to the office.

Before they even reached the door, it opened. A man emerged in a gray long sleeve dress shirt with a blue vest over it. Emblazoned on the vest was a golden crown, the storage company's logo. His head was completely shaved but for his eyebrows and a small goatee.

"Hey, you can't park there. Our customers have to be able to get in and out of the facility. You're blocking traffic. I'm going to have to ask you to move."

Bishop frowned. "No can do, Mr..."

"Jenkins," The man replied. "I'm the manager here."

Bishop flashed her ID. "Well, Mr. Jenkins, I'm Detective Bishop with the Ninth Precinct and we are investigating the bomb that just went off in Manhattan. We have reason to believe it may have been constructed in one of your sheds."

"That's ridiculous," Jenkins replied, shaking his head. "We have video surveillance and security twenty-four hours a day.

No one has been building bombs here."

"Does your surveillance cover what occurs within the storage units themselves?" Bishop asked.

"Of course not. Our customers value their privacy."

"Well, Jenkins. One of them used that privacy to build a bomb that just killed twenty people. Our investigators have dug up the suspect's credit card records and they show that a payment was made here in the last few days. So, we are going to need a look in his unit, and we're going to need you to evacuate the facility. We don't want anyone else getting injured or killed by this unhinged young man."

"What do you mean?" Jenkins asked.

Bishop towered over Jenkins as she answered him. "I mean, that at any moment, his storage here may explode."

CHAPTER 15

T he clerk looked at Bishop, his eyes wide and his jaw dropping. He didn't appear to know how to process what Bishop had just laid on him.

"That's right, explode," Kasey reiterated. "If you haven't seen the coverage on the news, you should. We have an apartment building that has been blasted over three city blocks. There hasn't been enough left of its occupants for us to even identify them yet. Unless you want to be his next victim, we need you to evacuate the facility and give us access to your records. We need to know which storage unit is his and we need to know now."

"I have an obligation to protect the privacy of my customers. I can't disclose that information without a warrant."

Bishop pointed to the bomb squad that were dismounting from their truck. "Mr. Jenkins, that's the bomb squad. They are here to secure any potential devices that our suspect may have created. If you don't tell us which storage unit belongs to Martin Langstrode, then they are going to go door-to-door sweeping them all. With or without your help. You can make the process a whole lot smoother, not to mention less dangerous to everyone involved, if you simply get on the computer and tell us what we want to know."

Jenkins studied the bomb squad as they dismounted. One of the officers was carrying a portable battering ram over his shoulder.

Jenkins nodded and backed into the office. He hurried around the desk and bent over the computer. As his hands touched the keyboard, he looked up at Bishop. "What did you say his name was?"

"Martin Langstrode," Kasey answered.

Jenkins began to type. After a few moments, he squinted at the screen. "According to our system, Martin rented unit C65. It's in the back on the right-hand side. What happens now?"

"You evacuate, Mr. Jenkins. We can't have anyone near that unit once the bomb squad enter. Do you have a PA system?"

"We do, but the speakers are scattered throughout the yard. There is no guarantee that everyone will hear them."

"It's better than nothing," Bishop replied. "Give it to me."

Martin picked up a transmitter from the counter and handed it to Bishop.

"This is Detective Bishop with the NYPD," she said. "Evacuate the facility. Cease what you're doing immediately and make your way to the front parking lot. Your life may be in danger. Please proceed swiftly to the evacuation area, now!"

Bishop handed the radio back to Jenkins. The clerk just stared at her blankly.

Kasey stepped passed the desk and put her arm around Jenkins. "Alright, Mr. Jenkins, time to go. You'll need to wait out front too."

She steered him out of the office, Bishop right behind her. When they reached the parking lot, the bomb squad was already assembled. A small machine on tracks was rolling its way across the parking lot toward them. The heavily armored bomb squad followed behind.

Bishop addressed the bomb squad. "Boys, the unit we want is C65. It's right in the back. If he is in there, he'll be able to see us coming. We have asked any other occupants to evacuate, so we have to watch out for other citizens making their way out. Keep your eyes peeled for Langstrode and proceed with caution. We have no idea if he is armed, but all indications are that he might be capable of creating other explosive devices. Proceed with care."

Kasey spotted some motion beside her. She looked to see Jenkins rummaging around in his pocket.

He pulled out a set of keys. "This is the master key. It should get you into the unit. If you can avoid knocking in the door, it would be greatly appreciated."

Bishop took the key and handed it to the lead officer. "Kasey and I will sweep the yard and keep our eyes peeled for anyone else leaving the storage sheds."

"Roger that, detective," The bomb squad's sergeant replied. "We'll take it from here."

The squad followed the bomb disposal robot as it rolled up to the gate.

"The black fob on the keychain, just wave it over the keypad," Jenkins shouted after them.

The officer found the fob and moments later, the gate rolled open.

Kasey and Bishop followed the bomb squad through the open gate and into the self-storage facility.

The storage facility consisted of row upon row of storage units, a veritable wall of concrete. Each unit was accessible only by a singular garaged door. The storage space was 10' x 18' by Kasey's estimation.

As they moved through the facility, Kasey spotted an open door.

"Bishop, up there on the right. The unit is open. Someone must be inside."

"It's not Martin's unit," Bishop replied. "Keep your eyes open. We have no idea who else is in here."

As they approached, a strange scratching emanated from the storage unit. It sounded like a wire being run along the surface of another object.

The bomb squad inched forward toward the open unit, officers fanning out as they approached. Ten feet. Six feet. Three feet.

The bomb squad halted.

"You have got to be kidding me," The lead officer declared.

"What is it?" Bishop asked, jogging toward them.

Kasey followed after her.

As they rounded the corner, a disheveled man in his twenties came into view. His brown hair was drawn back into a series of dreadlocks and he was holding an electric guitar plugged into a set of earphones. The man's eyes were closed, and he was strumming away as if his life depended on.

"That sound makes sense now," Bishop said.

The sound of the pick against the wires strings of the guitar is what Kasey had heard on her approach.

"You carry on, officers. We'll deal with this," Bishop replied.

Bishop entered the storage unit and inched toward the guitarist. Right as she was about to reach out and tap him, the man opened his eyes.

Leaping backward, he tripped over a cable and landed in a heap. The guitar bounced from his hands, as he struggled to catch it.

He ripped off his headphones. "Who the hell are you?"

Bishop simply raised her badge. "Detective Bishop, Ninth Precinct. I'm sure you missed the announcement due to your headphones, but there has been a bomb threat on the premises. You're currently standing near the blast zone. We are evacuating the facility so whatever you're doing here, you are going to have to pick it up later. We need you to make your way out to the parking lot immediately."

The man studied the badge as he struggled up off the ground. He went to set his guitar down but then turned to Bishop. "A bomb, you said?"

"That's right, shake a leg. We need you to get out here."

He nodded but instead of setting down his guitar, he unplugged it and took it with him. As he left the unit, Kasey called after him. "Why are you practicing in a storage unit? Surely you could do that at home."

He called over his shoulder, "I wish. The missus hates the thing. This is the only place I get any peace. Flaming bomb threat, it's just my luck."

His protests faded to a mumble as he disappeared up the driveway.

Kasey searched for any other open doors, but none were within sight. Leaving the musician's storage unit, she and Bishop followed after the bomb squad. They had set up in front of a unit some two hundred feet down the concourse.

As Kasey and Bishop followed them, an officer shouted, "That's close enough. Wait for us to secure the unit."

Kasey sighed turning to Bishop. "This isn't at all how I expected today to go."

"Tell me about it," Bishop replied. "That whole mess at the apartment. I've never seen anything like it. You see the stories on the news, but nothing prepares you for the real thing.

"Oh, come on, Bishop. I'm sure you've seen some horrendous homicides in your day," Kasey said.

"Most definitely, but I've never found a man's fingers blasted across Central Park. Before you arrived, we found three different fingers scattered over thirty square feet, it's like the world's worst game of Where's Wally, but you know what's worse, Kasey?"

"No, but I imagine you are going to tell me."

"Indeed, I am," Bishop replied. "We have no idea where the rest of him is. Parts of him could have landed three blocks away for all we know. Who does something like that? We spoke with Martin. He is barely in his twenties. Kasey, how does he go from graduating school to blowing up an apartment in less than ten years?"

"We don't know that he did," Kasey replied. "After all, I doubt he is a terrorist. More likely a terrified young man lashing out to protect his father."

Bishop nodded. "He could have been misled into making that bomb. There are plenty of sickos out there on the Internet who would have taught him this, just to create chaos and confusion here in the US. It is possible someone took advantage of him and inadvertently turned him into a mass murderer. We need more evidence or better yet, we need him in custody."

Kasey watched the bomb squad as they fussed about the entry to Martin's storage unit. One of the officers hunched over as he slid something under the door.

A camera, perhaps. They probably want to see if the place has been rigged to blow.

Kasey looked at Bishop. "Still no leads on his whereabouts?"

"This is it. We have an all-points bulletin out and we are watching for any activity on any of his credit cards or bank accounts. We're still scouring the street for leads too. Our officers are canvassing the neighborhood and checking surveillance footage to try and determine if and how he may have got out of the building. But it's no small feat. There are hundreds of cameras in the Upper East Side. If he got out, one of them will show up something eventually."

The bomb squad inserted Jenkin's key and rolled up the door of the storage unit. Several of the officers disappeared inside the unit.

After several minutes, the leader re-emerged and beckoned to Bishop. "Detective Bishop, you are gonna want to see this."

Kasey followed Bishop to the storage unit. Passing the bomb squad members waiting outside, Bishop and Kasey entered the shed.

The unit contained two lockers, both of which had been pried open by the bomb squad. There was little left within them. In the center of the storage unit was a workbench.

The top of the workbench was littered with paraphernalia. Several bricks of clay rested on the counter. It was a bizarre grey green mix that was unfamiliar to Kasey. Next to it there was a spool of wire. An array of electronic components rested on the bench. Beside the table a small tool set sat open.

"C4," Bishop said. "We suspected as much from the scene."

"Pardon?" Kasey raised an eyebrow.

"The explosive substance used in the blast was C4. We suspected as much but we were still waiting for the lab to confirm it. C4 is based on the military explosive RDX. Quite stable once it's been prepared and shaped. These bricks won't detonate without a shock wave from a detonator. There is still more than enough here to level this unit, though, and much of the facility," Bishop replied.

"Affirmative, detective," The bomb squad's sergeant replied. "But these are safe. None of the other blocks have detonators attached. We will take and dispose of them in due course, but you are in no immediate danger."

"Kasey and I will sweep the scene. There is more than enough explosive here for several blasts like we saw this morning. We need to determine where and how he might be using any remaining explosive devices. We also need evidence linking Martin to this unit. The credit card charge is something, but it's circumstantial. We need to be sure, and we need to know what his next move is."

Kasey set her kit down and opened the case. Pulling out a set of latex gloves, she slid them on and made her way over the workbench. Methodically, she bagged up each of the tools. They would provide a wealth of fingerprint evidence. Next, she collected the extraneous wires and spools that littered the table.

In short order, she cleared the desk of everything but the C4. As she went to turn away, the strange gray green blocks caught her eye. The bomb squad had said they would deal with them, but the bomb squad has said they had no detonators attached and were safe. Something in Kasey nagged at her.

Peeking over her shoulder, she verified no one was watching. The bomb squad had stepped outside to allow her to do her job and Bishop was pacing back and forth outside the unit.

Giving into her curiosity, Kasey reached out and gingerly picked up the brick of C4.

As her hand clasped around it, the hairs on the back of her neck stood up.

Oh, no. It's going to blow.

No explosion came but a familiar mist descended, clouding her vision.

When the mist cleared, Kasey found herself surrounded by darkness. The only illumination came from a small strip of light running in a line before her. As her eyes adjusted to the dark, she realized she was in a room. To her left, she could hear the jingling noise of metal against metal.

Keys.

Her guess proved correct as she heard the familiar ring of a key sliding into a lock. The lock released, and the entire wall began to move.

It's the roller door. I'm in the storage unit.

As light flooded the room, she had to blink to drive away the blinding glare. The setting sun was streaming straight in the open door of the storage unit.

When Kasey's eyes adjusted to the blinding light, she could see a figure standing in the door. It was a man, muscular and well over six feet tall. His hair was a light shade of brown which blended almost seamlessly into his well-trimmed beard. He wore a black leather jacket and carried a black duffel bag.

The man entered the storage unit. Making his way to a workbench in the center of the unit, he sat down the duffel. Kasey watched eagerly as he unzipped it and proceeded to unload its contents. The man took out what appeared to be several textbooks and some women's clothes and set them on the counter. Then he rummaged about inside the duffel for a few moments before looking at where Kasey stood.

Kasey's heart skipped a beat, but nothing happened. The man just went back to his work.

He can't see me. Of course not. I'm not really here.

She wondered, and not for the first time, if those she observed in a vision had any inkling of her presence or if she was simply a silent voyeur of their life.

She watched as the man lifted several of the bricks of C4 off the table and gently placed them inside the bag. As he did so, he layered clothes and textbooks inside the duffel.

He's hiding the bomb.

As Kasey watched him pack the bag, she noticed a tattoo on his forearm. It was a heart with a knife through it. Running down each side was a lightning bolt.

The man lifted one last brick of C4 off the table and held it aloft. Kasey realized it was three smaller bricks that had been strapped together. On top of the bricks was a cell phone fastened to a series of wires.

That must be the detonator, Kasey thought. The phone must allow them to trigger it remotely.

Kasey watched as the remaining clothes and textbooks were placed into the duffel. The man zipped the bag before raising it off the table and swinging it over his shoulder. He surveyed the unit one last time, then turned and left. As he left he stood on his toes and pulled down the storage unit's garage door. The steel door scraped down its runners until it collided with the concrete. There was a clang and a jangle of keys as the stranger locked the unit, leaving Kasey in darkness once more. Then, as suddenly as it began, the vision ended.

As the mist cleared, Kasey found herself standing in the storage unit once more.

She looked down at the workbench and realized she was still holding the brick of C4 in her hand. Before she could place it back on the table, a voice from the doorway called.

"Ma'am, you need to put that down. It may not have a detonator but it's still an explosive device. We have no indication yet as to who made it or where it was purchased from. That much C4 could level the storage unit and everything else for fifty feet. So please pop it back on the table, gently."

Kasey set the brick of C4 back on the workbench. "I'm sorry, I was just collecting evidence."

"No need," the officer replied. "We'll take a sample before we dispose of it."

Kasey nodded. "Of course."

Bishop's eyes caught Kasey. She must have read Kasey's surprised expression because she immediately strode toward her.

When she was close enough to not be overheard, she whispered, "What happened? What did you see?"

"How do you know?" Kasey asked.

Bishop smiled. "When you picked up the C4, you went still. You were staring at it but not moving. I recognized the vacant expression on your face. I'd seen it before. The same thing happened to you at Beth's crime scene, right?"

Kasey raised an eyebrow. "Yeah, it did. I saw a vision of Brad and Beth arguing. That's why I was so determined that it was him."

"That makes much more sense now," Bishop said. "I don't know what control you have over it, but you might want to work on that vacant stare. It's a bit of a giveaway. Not that people are going to guess what's happening, but well, it's unsettling. They may think you are doing drugs or just a weirdo. That's the real danger, I guess."

"Hey!" Kasey exclaimed placing her hands on her hips in mock outrage.

"Never mind that," Bishop replied with a wave of her hand. "What did you see?"

"I saw a vision of this place." Her mind raced as she tried to recall and process the vivid details of the vision. "You talked to the building manager at the apartments, right?"

"That's right," Bishop replied. "That's how we got onto Martin in the first place. The building manager saw him carrying a duffel bag into the elevator, minutes before the explosion. The manager thought he was up to something."

"I don't think he made the bomb," Kasey answered. "In my vision, I saw a man packing the explosives into a duffel. It could be the same bag. In my vision he was also loading other things into it. Textbooks, clothes, a whole heap of junk. I don't think Martin had any idea what he was carrying. If he did, why bother going to all that extra effort? It's not like there is a bag check at the apartment entrance."

"So, the man you saw wasn't Martin?" Bishop asked.

"Nope. Definitely not that weedy little drug dealer. The man I saw was massive. Easily six-foot three and he was rocking a full beard. There's no way it was Martin. No disguise is that good."

"So he's working with someone?" Bishop asked.

"I think it's more likely he was working for someone and just didn't know it," Kasey replied. "The bomb had a cell phone strapped to it. I think that's how they detonated the blast. I don't think Martin had any idea, and once we finish gathering evidence at the apartments, I think we're going to find that Martin never made it out. We need to find the real bomber."

Bishop nodded. "A cell phone, you say? An interesting choice. Normally, people would choose a radio detonator. We'll run through telecom records for any calls placed to or from the area immediately before the detonation. I'm sure that phone was obliterated, but if we can work out where the call was placed from, it may give us a lead. In the meantime, I need to get you back to the station. Team up with a sketch artist and get working on an image of this guy for the evening news. We need to find him as soon as possible."

"What are you going to do?" Kasey asked.

Bishop pointed at the slowly descending afternoon sun. "I'm gonna drop you off at the station and then I'm going for a swim. I need to work off some of this steam. Don't worry, I'll be back. I have a feeling it's going to be a long night. Pack your kit and let's go."

Kasey strode back to the workbench and loaded all the samples she had gathered into her kit. Closing the lid, she hefted it off the table and followed Bishop.

Bishop turned to the bomb squad. "Okay, boys, it's all yours. Thanks for your help today."

"No worries, Bishop. We'll deal with this ordnance and let you know if we come up with anything you can use to track down the bomber."

"Much appreciated," Bishop said with a wave.

Kasey and Bishop made their way back to the car park where Jenkins was pacing back and forth.

When he saw Bishop, he stopped. "Did you find anything, detective?"

"Sure did, Jenkins. Enough C4 to turn your storage units into a new swimming pool for the city. The bomb squad is dealing with it now. You should be safe to return to work shortly." Bishop tossed the manager's keys back to him.

He clutched at the keys as they slipped through his fingers before landing on the asphalt.

Bishop glanced around the car park. As Kasey followed her gaze, she realized what Bishop was looking for.

"Jenkins?" Bishop began.

"Yes, detective?" He replied as he scooped up his keys.

"Those cameras are real, right?"

Jenkins averted his gaze. "Two of them are. The ones that are watching the gate. The others are fakes. You know as well as I do, that every deterrent helps keep thieves away."

"Indeed they do, and perhaps the real ones will help us catch our bomber. I want a copy of your footage from the day that unit was first rented until now. Send it over to the Ninth Precinct."

"Yes, detective. I'll send it at once."

Bishop turned to Kasey "All right, you ready to roll?"

"Sure am," Kasey replied. "We've got a bomber to catch, and now we know precisely what he looks like."

CHAPTER 16

After working with the sketch artist Kasey headed downstairs to the morgue. As she walked, Kasey tapped her phone against her palm. Spotting his light that was still on, she headed for Vida's office.

Vida looked up from his computer. "How did it go? What did our boy look like?"

Kasey pulled up her email on her phone. Tony's likeness had already come through. Tapping on the image, she blew it up, so that it occupied the whole screen. She walked over to Vida and sat down beside him.

"Meet our bomber, Vida. This is the man responsible for packing the explosives that blew up the Fifth Avenue apartments."

"Martin was just collateral damage?" Vida asked.

"Seems like it," Kasey replied

"What's his connection to the family?" Vida asked.

Kasey brushed her hair back out of her face. "No idea. All I saw was him packing the bag. I have no clue what would motivate him to blow up the building. The blast killed Martin and Cynthia along with many others. We're still waiting for the results of the evidence we gathered from the scene."

"Any chance the bombing was another hit gone wrong? Maybe Cynthia hired more than one guy and things went off course."

Kasey shrugged. "It's always possible. It seems pretty sloppy, though, taking out their own employer. Doesn't seem like a very effective business model. She only paid the shooter half up front. I'm sure she would have followed a similar pattern with other hired guns. It would also be foolish to blow up an apartment when you aren't even sure if your target is inside. I think it's safe to say, whoever our bomber is, he wasn't working for Cynthia."

Vida tapped his pen against the desk. "What if he is working for Mr. Langstrode? Maybe it was revenge for the attempted shooting yesterday?

"Perhaps." Kasey nodded. "But that's cold, having his own son carry the bomb in. Do you think he is capable of that?"

Vida shook his head. "I really don't know, Kasey. You've spoken to him more than me, but from what I've read, he's a ruthless business partner. It's not much of a leap to think he'd kill in the name of self-preservation. If he thinks Cynthia is out to kill him, I could see him being motivated enough to try something like this."

"It's possible," Kasey said. "We will have to have a chat with Mr. Langstrode and see what he's been up to. We know the bomb was detonated by a phone call. Bishop's having the tech guys look into it. If we can track who placed that call, we'll have our bomber."

Vida leaned back in his chair. "So, what's our play?"

Kasey stretched. "While we wait, I want to have a look through our database. Our bomb maker had a tattoo on his left arm. I want to know if it means anything."

She thought of the Shinigami and the tattoo that had given away their acolytes. The warning had come just in time to save her life. Perhaps the marking on the bomb makers arm might prove significant, too.

"I don't know. Give me a rough sketch, and I can dig through the database and see what we've got," Vida replied. "If I come up with anything I'll let you know."

Kasey grabbed a pen and piece of paper on the desk and doodled the tattoo. She pushed the paper toward him "Thanks, Vida, you're a champion. I'm going to duck upstairs and have a chat with our friend, Mr. Langstrode. I want to hear what he has to say about working with the Ainsleys. He was pretty keen to keep that little tidbit concealed earlier. I want to know why."

"No worries. I'll get to work."

Kasey slid out of her chair and made her way to the elevator. Riding it up to the second-floor lounge, she pondered on how she would approach Sal. He'd been unwilling to reveal his business partner before. Kasey wondered how he would react to Vida having uncovered the truth.

When the elevator doors opened, she stepped out into the lounge. It was empty but for an officer sitting at the table, chowing down on a sub.

Langstrode was gone.

Kasey's heart skipped a beat. She rushed over to the officer. "Have you seen the man that was here earlier? Langstrode. He had a protective detail. Two officers around the clock. Where has he gone? Where is his detail?"

The officer swallowed the bite of his sub before clearing his throat.

"He's been gone for hours. It was shortly after news of the bomb blast spread. He left the station. Said something about his wife being dead. He figured he didn't need any more protection. He told us he couldn't stay cooped up here indefinitely. Hired some muscle and left to go back to work."

Hired some muscle. Kasey thought. Oh, no.

Were they the same as the ones in her vision? She ran back to the elevator, but it was already gone.

No time to waste.

She sprinted for the stairs. Taking them two at a time, she was in the lobby in no time. She threw open the station's large double doors and stepped out onto the street. Picking up her cell, she tried to call Langstrode. There was no answer.

She punched out a text to him, instead. "Sal, it's Kasey. Call me as soon as you get this. You are still in danger."

She paced back and forth in front of the station, unsure what to do.

Her phone vibrated.

New message received.

Kasey opened the message; it was from Sal. It read, "Don't worry, Kasey, got my own security. Your officers are busy enough as it is."

Accompanying the text was a picture. Kasey opened the picture to see Sal standing between two burly bodyguards. The men wore suits with no ties. Kasey recognized them immediately. They were the men from her vision.

Hell. Kasey went to dial Langstrode's number, but before she could, her phone began to ring.

She looked at the caller ID. It was a blocked number.

She answered the phone, raising it to her ear.

Her heart pounded, her palms sweating as city traffic passed her by. Sal Langstrode was walking to his death, the same fate she'd witnessed in her vision, and she couldn't reach him.

"Hello," she said.

"Miss Chase. It's good to speak with you."

She scowled. "Who is this? How did you get my number?"

"That doesn't really matter, Miss Chase. All that matters now is this: no doubt that message you got was our friend, Mr. Langstrode."

"I don't know what you're talking about," she stammered.

"No need to lie to me, Miss Chase. It's written all over your face."

Kasey looked up. They are watching me.

She scanned the street, but there were people everywhere— pedestrians, bike messengers, and people in the cars passing by. No less than a dozen buildings offered a vantage point to where she now stood.

"No need to look up, Miss Chase. I'm right here. Right in front of you."

Kasey's eyes darted down, focusing across the street where she spotted a towering hulk of a man. His bulging biceps seemed liable to burst through his tight T-shirt. His strong angular jaw and well-trimmed beard were instantly recognizable. It was the bomber.

As Kasey locked eyes with him, he smiled.

Kasey's jaw dropped, and she took a step forward toward the street.

"Oh, no, Miss Chase. You don't want to be doing that. This is as close as you come. After all, you have no idea who you're dealing with. This little backpack I'm carrying has enough explosives to clear the street. If you take so much as one more step in my direction, I'll blow it. You may be bold, but I don't think you're willing to risk the lives of everyone on this street. Besides, I've come with news. If you don't hear me out, it's going to have dire repercussions for those closest to you."

"What do you mean?" Kasey asked.

The bomber smiled. "What I'm saying is that you have two choices, Miss Chase. We both know where Mr. Langstrode is heading now. He is about to die, and you are going to let it happen."

Kasey shook her head. "Why would I do that?"

"Because, Miss Chase, Detective Bishop is enjoying her evening swim. In a couple of minutes, she will climb out of the pool, towel herself off, take a brief shower, and get in her car. The moment she does, the bomb beneath it will kill her and anyone within twenty feet of it. You could always try and save Mr. Langstrode, but if you aren't there to stop Bishop before she gets into her car, she is dead. Your choice, Miss Chase."

"I'm going to find you," Kasey said, "and when I do—"

"You'll do nothing," the bomber interrupted. "I'll always be three steps ahead of you. Now drop your phone into the trash can to your right. Now."

"My phone?" Kasey asked,

"Of course. I don't want you getting any ideas or calling anyone else. If you care about Bishop, you need to throw your phone in the trash and get moving."

Kasey lowered her phone and looked at. Across the road, the bomber stood silently waiting.

Kasey gritted her teeth. I'm going to kill you.

She hurled the phone into the trash and looked back across the street. The bomber flashed her a smile and waved.

There was nothing else she could do. The bomber held all the pieces.

It was Bishop or Langstrode.

Her vision hadn't warned her about this. Saving Langstrode's life came at a price. That price was detective Bishop.

Diane.

Her partner and friend. It was a price she just wasn't willing to pay.

Sorry, Sal.

She turned west and ran.

CHAPTER 17

K asey ran for all she was worth. She knew that Bishop swam at the local rec center. It was one of the few heated pools that were affordable on a budget.

Bishop lived on a schedule. As Kasey ran, she prayed Bishop was running late. It was ten to six. Bishop would be out of the pool any minute.

Pedestrians looked at her in surprise as she dashed past them. She hit Second Avenue and turned left, her mind racing. Sprinting down the sidewalk, she considered trying to borrow someone's cell phone.

Perhaps she could ring the station and have them send someone after Langstrode.

They'll never get there in time. Sal was with the guards she had seen in her vision, it was possible they were already at the construction site. The bomber had certainly sounded confident enough. What if Kasey wasted time arguing with a random person over their phone only to find that Bishop had finished early?

Kasey turned west onto East Fourth Street. The last few weeks had exhausted her. She had barely been able to make it to the gym, and her once regular runs had become few and far between. She sucked in a deep breath as she tried to pace herself. She was out of shape and she could feel it. Weaving through the pedestrians, she didn't break her stride.

What impact would abandoning Sal have on the fate of the city? With Vida's research, she was sure that the building at Park Avenue lay at the heart of what was to come. Clearly the attack emanated from the structure. She had seen as much in her vision. Somehow, the Shinigami would use it as a staging ground to level the city.

If Vida's conclusions about the attack were correct, the devastation would be cataclysmic. Most of Manhattan would be completely destroyed. Millions would die. The resulting tectonic impact would ripple outward, devastating most of the surrounding city.

The tidal events were harder to predict. After the earthquake in Chile, tsunamis had devastated much of the Pacific. With the earthquake occurring in Manhattan, the eastern seaboard of the United States would be annihilated. The death toll would be catastrophic. The weight of so many lives weighed heavily on Kasey's shoulders as she ran to save Bishop.

Would saving her friend jeopardize the lives of countless others? Would Bishop even want that if she knew?

Bishop was selfless, more than happy to put her life on the line to save others. That's why she'd become a police officer. There was no way she would want Kasey prioritizing her life above so many others. Kasey knew it.

But I'm not Bishop. There was also no way to know whether saving Sal would result in the city being destroyed or prevent it. Sal could be part of the entire plot.

I need more information.

She passed New York University and Washington Square Park, puffing heavily as she powered on. She could feel the buildup of lactic acid in her leg muscles as she turned left onto Washington Square Way. Winding to her right, she checked for traffic. As soon as there was a slight gap, she sprinted across the road. She couldn't afford to wait for the crossing signals.

Turning right, she ran up the lane way. As she reached Sixth Avenue, she let out a sigh of relief. The streetlight was red, but the crossing signal flashed green. It would change any moment. She picked up her pace, pushing out a deep breath as she crossed the street.

A man in a suit stepped sideways unexpectedly, right into her path. With all her momentum she struck him like a runaway train. The man spun and hit the sidewalk. Kasey wanted to stop but couldn't afford to.

"Sorry!" she shouted over her shoulder.

The man cursed after her, but she didn't have time for nonsense. Instead, she darted down Carmine street. The rec center was at the end of the street. She only hoped she was in time. With grim determination, she pressed on in spite of the cold sweat running down her face. Her hair flew wildly about her.

I must have made it in time.

If a bomb had gone off, there would be more commotion. Kasey glanced left as she cut across Bedford Street, narrowly avoiding being run down by a taxi. She was almost there.

"Bishop, where are you?" Kasey muttered to herself.

As she reached Seventh Avenue, she looked up to see Bishop coming through the front door of the rec center. The street was packed with traffic, but she had no choice.

"Bishop!" Kasey shouted as she leapt into the street.

She wove between the traffic, all the while shouting at Bishop.

Bishop didn't respond. The wires sticking out from beneath Bishop's sandy blonde hair were to blame.

Oh, no, she's wearing earphones. She can't hear me.

Bishop descended the stairs and set out across the sidewalk. Kasey spotted Bishop's car parked right beside the center. Bishop crossed the sidewalk, heading straight for the driver's side door

"Bishop!" Kasey screamed again as she cleared the street.

Bishop stopped, and Kasey thought she'd gotten through to her friend. Unfortunately, Bishop was just looking for her keys. After fishing them out of her purse, she unlocked the car.

Kasey was almost there, but Bishop reached for the handle.

Out of time, Kasey leapt.

As Bishop's hand grasped the door handle, Kasey struck her hard, tackling Bishop to the pavement. Both of them hit the ground hard. They rolled across the pavement until they came to a halt.

Kasey grit her teeth, as her arms and elbows took the brunt of the blow.

"What the—" Bishop began, before realizing who had tackled her. "Kasey, what are you doing here?"

Kasey tried to suck in a deep breath. She was out of wind. The run had been punishing but hitting the concrete had driven the last of her breath from her. Unable to speak, she pointed feebly toward the car.

"Talk to me, Kasey. What's going on? What about the car?"

"It...has...been...rigged." Kasey struggled to breathe. "There's a bomb."

From where she was resting on the sidewalk, Kasey could see that the bomber wasn't lying. Fastened underneath the driver's side of the vehicle was a brick of C4. It was wired to another device. While Kasey wasn't positive, she supposed it was a pressure switch, designed to detonate the bomb as soon as Bishop had sat down.

She had only just made it in time. Seconds later and Bishop would have been blown to pieces. Whoever the bomber was, he was willing to kill anyone who got in his way.

Bishops gaze followed Kasey's finger. "A bomb. What on earth? How did you know?"

"There's no time for that," Kasey replied. "You need to speak with dispatch. Langstrode is on his way to the building now. He's going to die, Bishop."

"What do you mean? I thought he was at the station," Bishop replied as she rolled onto her back and struggled to her feet.

Kasey winced as she got up. "No. He got tired of waiting, so he hired his own security and went back to work. I saw them, though. They are the men from my vision. His own security are the ones that throw him off the building. It's going to happen now. I just know it."

"Then why are you here? Why didn't you go after them?" Bishop shook her fist.

"I saw the bomber," Kasey stammered. "He gave me a choice. Go after Langstrode or try to save you. He is how I knew your car was rigged. He had me toss my phone in the trash. It was you or Langstrode. I had to make a choice."

Bishop looked at the bomb. "I'm glad you did, Kasey." She squeezed Kasey tight. "I owe you my life, but we need to do something about Langstrode." Bishop dusted herself off and pulled out her phone, waving off pedestrians and gym-goers who were gathering about.

Kasey recognized the station's phone number at a glance.

"It's Detective Bishop," Bishop said into the phone. "We have an urgent request for dispatch. We have reason to believe that Langstrode is in grave danger. He is on his way to the construction site at 432 Park Avenue. We need any units in the area to head there immediately. Take Langstrode back into protective custody and arrest anyone who is with him."

Kasey couldn't make out the muffled response.

"What do you mean they are already on site?" Bishop paced and nodded. "I see. Have them secure the scene. We will be there as soon as we can. Meanwhile, I need you to raise the bomb squad. We are at the corner of Seventh Avenue and Clarkson Street. Someone has fitted an explosive device to my car. I can't leave it unattended in case someone else sets it off. We need them at once."

Bishop hung up the phone.

"What's going on?" Kasey asked.

"We are too late. Langstrode is already dead. Officers are on scene already. Someone called 911 when they saw someone jump off the building. It's Langstrode. Our officers are locking down the scene now."

Kasey sunk her head into her hands.

"We are too late," she muttered.

Bishop sat down beside her. "There's nothing you could have done, Kasey. Langstrode was already with them. Even if you'd gone after them, they would have killed him anyway."

Kasey fought back tears. "For days, we have known what was going to happen. We had him, and we let him slip through our fingers and now he's dead. What good is seeing the future if I can't do a damn thing to stop it? He is dead because of me."

Bishop put her arm around Kasey. "You can't beat yourself up about this, Kasey. You didn't kill him, they did. Because of you, I'm alive. Not to mention all the other people that bomb would have killed. You can't let this get to you."

A tear rolled down Kasey's cheek. "You know that smug little mongrel had the stones to confront me in front of the police station. Bold as brass, not a care in the world. Knew I wasn't going to do anything because he had a bag full of C4. We need to find him, Bishop. We need to find him and put him down before he can hurt anyone else."

Bishop patted her on the back. "Don't worry, he is as good as dead, but in the mean time we need to clear this street. That bomb is still dangerous."

Kasey brushed herself off. She hurt all over.

Bishop pulled out her badge and waved it in the air.

"Alright people we need you to back up," she shouted toward the parking lot. "Give us some space. You are all in grave danger."

The spectators went from curious to concerned.

"She means that, folks," Kasey added. "Back it up. We are waiting for the bomb squad. None of you want to be here, trust me."

The crowd began whispering.

"Did she say bomb?" a woman asked.

"That's right people, a bomb. Now get out here," Kasey shouted.

The mass of people scattered in every direction.

Bishop shook her head. "Normally, we try to avoid causing a panic."

Kasey looked both ways. "You said you wanted to clear the street. It's cleared. Enough people have died today."

As Kasey waited for the approaching sirens to arrive, her mind kept returning to Langstrode and her earlier vision of him plummeting to his death.

I'm sorry Sal.

CHAPTER 18

The mood in the morgue was even more somber than usual. The bomb squad had managed to defuse the device attached to Bishop's car but by the time Kasey and Bishop had made it to Park Avenue, there had been nothing left to do. The coroner had already removed Langstrode's body. To their surprise, both security guards had also been found dead at the scene.

Both had been shot dead by a small caliber pistol at close range. They too had been removed. Kasey had examined the scene, hoping to see another vision but nothing came. Clearly her gift had already shown her all it had to offer concerning Sal's demise.

Is this what I get for ignoring its warning?

The dead security guards were yet another lesson as to how much she had missed in her earlier vision. As she thought back, Kasey could now remember the gunshots as Langstrode had plummeted to his death. It was only now that she understood their purpose. Clearly the guards had been expendable muscle. Another loose end being tied up by the meticulous bomber.

Kasey plonked herself down in a stool and stared at the white board. Bishop too pulled up a chair, its legs grinding across the tiles. She sat down with a heavy sigh.

"Kasey, is that you?" a voice called. It was Vida from his office.

"Yeah, Vida, it's me. Bishop's here too. What are you still doing here? It's late. You should be asleep by now."

Vida burst out of his office, a roll of paper clenched in his hand. "I've been calling you for hours." Vida took in Kasey and Bishop's disheveled appearance. "Where have you been? You look awful."

Kasey leaned back in the chair. Her grazed elbows rubbed on the armrests as she did, pain shooting up her arms. "Thanks, Vida. I know I can always rely on you to make me feel better."

"What happened?" Vida asked.

Kasey winced as she studied her grazed arms. "Our bomber friend rigged Bishop's car to blow. I only just made it in time, but the sidewalk got the better of me."

"That's no good. Did you bust up your phone in the process?"

"No." Kasey sighed. "It's in the trashcan out front, or at least it was. Seems like it's been emptied in the last few hours."

Vida raised an eyebrow. "Why did you toss your phone?"

"It wasn't my choice," Kasey replied. "The bomber confronted me in front of the station. He threatened to blow up the street if I didn't toss my phone and go after Bishop. I didn't have much of a choice. He's already shown that he's more than willing to kill innocent people. I couldn't take the chance. Now I'm down a phone and I feel like hell. But when I get my hands on him, he is going to wish he was never born."

"Well, that may be sooner than you think," Vida replied, waving the papers he was carrying. "That's what I've been calling you about. I think I know who he is."

Bishop sat upright. "How?"

Vida glowed with pride. "I've been digging into the tattoo that Kasey saw in her vision. It's pretty distinct and it seems to have been showing up increasingly over the past eighteen months. Not down here, mainly further up north. Several of the northern precincts have reported interactions with a new crew. That tattoo is their insignia."

"Who are they?" Bishop asked.

"Bleeding hearts," Vida said. "According to our colleagues up north, they took over the northern suburbs, forcing the Dominicans toward the East River. They seem to primarily operate out of Inwood."

"What's their racket? Guns? Drugs? Girls?" Bishop asked.

"Drugs," Vida answered with a grin. "You can think of them as a more militant Walter White. They are believed to be behind a large crystal meth manufacturing empire. Several of their known associates have done or are doing time for possession or dealing.

"Unfortunately, the crew themselves seem to keep their noses pretty clean. The DEA and local precincts have been working up a case against them, but the case is still fairly circumstantial. They run a series of legitimate businesses that the DRA believe is laundering their money. There are a number of bars, a casino, a car wash, two laundromats, and most recently a marina."

"A marina?" Bishop asked tapping her foot impatiently. "That's a little unusual. The others make sense: a steady flow of cash business makes it easy to smuggle money in and launder it through the businesses. The marina, though. Certainly unusual."

"Why is that?" Kasey asked.

"It's a luxury business," Bishop said. "The purchase and sale of boats are larger transactions. Anything in that ballpark gets reported due to anti-money laundering provisions. It doesn't make a lot of sense for them to add it to their operation, that's all."

"Until you consider its place on the Hudson," Vida replied while digging through his paperwork to produce a printed map. "I doubt they are using it to launder their cash. It is far more likely that it serves as a distribution hub. The Hudson has quick and easy access to most of New York. On its West

Bank, you have New Jersey, and if the vessel is substantial enough, most of the East Coast of the United States. It's likely that the marina is a front to allow them to move their product more smoothly. The port of New York is far too heavily overseen after the recent crackdowns on organized crime. Owning a private marina is actually pretty clever when you think about it."

"Yes, I'd feel like applauding their business acumen, if they weren't so busy trying to blow us up," Kasey replied clenching her fists. "How do they even fit into this whole mess? What do the Bleeding Hearts want with the Langstrodes?"

"I wondered that myself," Vida said. "Until I found the bomber. He has been very busy lately."

"You have a name?" Bishop asked. "Give it to me."

"It's Dante Hossack. The 34th precinct have had dealings with him in the past. Once I knew which crew the tattoo belonged to, it was only a matter of time. I ran Kasey's likeness through our system and compared it to the records of all known Bleeding Hearts that we have on file. Dante is the closest match."

"You're sure?" Bishop asked her eyes shone hopefully.

"Positive. The likeness wasn't perfect, but I took the mug shot from the 34th Precinct and ran with that. As you know, I've been digging through the surveillance footage from the Fifth Avenue bombing. The supervisor sent over weeks' worth of footage. Martin may have entered the building minutes before the blast, but you'll never guess who else made frequent visits to those apartments."

"You're kidding?" Bishop said. "The bomber visited the scene before he blew it up. What is that? Some sort of sick fetish?"

"Oh, no," Vida said, smiling. The head ME was clearly thrilled with himself. "He was there visiting someone. The one member of the Langstrode family we all took for granted."

"Alicia," Kasey replied. "She's in cahoots with our bomber? Why would she do something like that?"

Vida shook his head. "Apparently, she has a taste for the bad boys. Dante may be almost ten years older than her, but apparently, he made quite the impression. I put in a call to the apartment manager. He's been visiting regularly for the last three months. More importantly, he picked Alicia up from the building the night before the blast."

"You think the bombing was some sort of sick gesture to keep his girlfriend safe?" Bishop asked.

Kasey thought about what Vida was saying. The bomber's identity brought everything together. She sprang her feet and picked up the white board marker. She hurriedly drew crosses through each of the names on the board.

"What are you doing?" Bishop asked.

Kasey drew a large circle around Alicia's name. "She's not the innocent daughter we thought she was. She's the one surviving Langstrode. More importantly, she is the only one left alive who has anyplace in Sal's will. We know that Martin was written out months ago after his arrest. Cynthia, doubtless, was removed shortly after the attempted assassination the other night. Not that it matters, now that she is dead. With Sal murdered this evening, Alicia is the only one left to enjoy the inheritance. She had her father killed. She has likely been planning it the whole time.

"Her mother and brother were wiped out in the bombing. I bet if we track the call that was placed to detonate the explosive, we'll find it came from her. With her mother and brother out of the picture, she was free to kill her own father. She is eighteen, there is nothing to prevent her receiving her inheritance now. She'll be set up for the rest of her life."

"But where do the Bleeding Hearts fit in?" Bishop asked.

"I think they supplied the muscle," Kasey replied, putting the lid back on the marker.

"In exchange for what?" Bishop countered "Some money? I doubt that. They already have substantial assets from what Vida was indicating."

"No doubt they have plenty of cash," Kasey replied. "Drug dealers always do. But you said it yourself they have to launder all their cash before they can do anything substantial with it. Vida, do you still have that list of Langstrode's assets, and those of his companies? I'm willing to bet my life that somewhere in the Langstrode estate there is a property or development in Inwood."

Vida's eyes lit up. "There is. Langstrode and his company recently acquired a stretch of the riverfront with development approval to build luxury apartments. The land alone is worth tens of millions of dollars. Langstrode was able to secure the land when it was released by the city. It used to be a park until it was rezoned and sold."

"What's the bet that our friend Ainsley helped facilitate that in exchange for Langstrode's help at Park Avenue?" Kasey asked.

"Seems more than likely," Bishop replied.

The sound of a throat being cleared interrupted their discussion. Kasey looked up to see someone standing in the doorway of the morgue.

"Chief West. What are you doing down here?" Kasey asked.

The chief strolled into the room. "I heard about your car, Bishop. I'm just glad you're alright."

"Thanks, chief." Bishop gave a weary smile. "Kasey got to me just in time."

"So I heard. The real question is what are you all doing down here? What's all this?" He pointed at the white board.

"We're trying to work out who is responsible for the bombing this morning, and for rigging my car this afternoon. It turns out that it's related to our case with Langstrode."

"I heard he died tonight. Thrown off a building. I'm sorry to hear that," the chief said. "An ugly way to go. What does the bomber have to do with it?"

"Short answer," Bishop said. "Our bomber is a member of a group moving drugs along the Hudson. It seems one of their ringleaders is shacked up with Langstrode's daughter. They knocked off the old man in order to get her inheritance early. It's likely they are being paid off with some prime real estate in Inwood."

"You have enough evidence to prove that?" the chief asked.

"Yes!" Kasey replied.

Bishop was more reserved. Tilting her head to one side, she admitted, "Almost. We have a positive ID on our bomber, we know he rigged my car and the device that blew up the luxury apartments. That alone is enough to send him down for life. For the daughter, well, so far, we only have conjecture, but we've already requested the cell phone records. I imagine once we run those, we'll find evidence linking her to the bomb that killed her brother and mother. We know the bomb was detonated by a phone call. If we trace that phone call to Alicia or any of her friends in the Bleeding Hearts, then we will have her too."

Chief West nodded slowly. "That's fine work. Do you know where we can find these Bleeding Hearts?"

"We have the addresses of several of their businesses in Inwood," Kasey replied. "The DEA has also been building a case. I'm sure that they will have others."

"Excellent," the chief replied. "Get a list of every address you have to me in ten minutes. Have the DEA send over anything that they wish to add."

"Add?" Bishop asked.

"To the warrant," the chief replied. "These little beggars blew up an apartment today and killed twenty-two people, that we know of so far. More than that, they tried to kill you, Bishop. We've lost too many good officers lately. These people think they can kill NYPD officers and get away with it. They need to be taught that such conduct won't be tolerated. Get me the addresses. I'll have Judge Rawlings issue a warrant tonight."

"It's late, Chief. I doubt the judge will be in Chambers," Bishop replied.

"It's a good thing I have his home number then, isn't it?" the chief replied. "He owes me a favor. He'll forgive the intrusion.

Liaise with the DEA and ready the list. We'll raid every address in their organization, and we'll do it tonight. While they are busy resting on their laurels, we'll hit them at home. They'll never come after one of us again and it will send a message to anyone else who is considering it. Any questions?"

Kasey and Bishop shook their head. The chief was on the warpath, and Kasey ready to let him run straight over Dante Hossack and the Bleeding Hearts.

"Get me that list, and run down the trace on the daughter's cell," the Chief called as he headed for the door. "Then grab whatever rest you can. It's going to be a long night."

CHAPTER 19

K asey adjusted her bullet-proof vest for the third time. They had traced Alicia's phone to the marina. Now a joint task force of the NYPD and DEA were en-route. Kasey and Bishop were riding with the chief, the three of them were sitting in the tactical unit's armored truck. A dozen other squad cars followed close behind.

The mood in the armored truck was tense as the officers of the Ninth Precinct prepared for a direct assault on the Bleeding Hearts headquarters.

Chief West had come through. Judge Rawlings had issued a warrant authorizing the search of the marina along with a dozen other suspected Bleeding Heart operations. The judge had been reluctant at first, but on hearing of the gang's connection with the Fifth Avenue bombing, he'd promptly issued the warrant.

It was three am. Most of Inwood was asleep as the convoy wove silently through the streets. There were no lights and no sirens. There would be no warning for the Bleeding Hearts. No mercy for Dante Hossack

The chief reached for the radio. "Alright, officers. You know the drill. We are sixty seconds out. The tactical teams will breach the marina and proceed to sweep the facility. The trailing officers will form a perimeter to ensure no one escapes the marina. We have a vessel in the water to prevent any escape along the Hudson. But remember, these aren't your run-of-the-mill thugs. They are organized and heavily armed, and they have shown themselves capable of improvising explosive devices. So be on the lookout for anything suspicious. These guys came after one of our own. If they draw a weapon, put them in the ground. Any questions?"

"No, chief!" was the resounding response.

A voice crackled over the radio. "Chief, we're approaching the gates."

The chief pushed transmit on his radio. "Take them down. Those gates won't keep us out."

"Understood," the voice said. "Hold on tight. Ten seconds to impact."

Kasey counted in her head. One, two, three.

As she hit eight, the vehicle sped up. The truck engine let out a rumble.

There was a deafening crash as the armored personnel carrier slammed through the steel gates of the marina. The truck hit its brakes, its tires screeching across the asphalt as it came to a halt.

"Go, go, go," the Chief shouted. "Squad A, sweep to the left. Sweep the structures one by one until you've cleared the boat sheds. Squad B, you have the cafe and the pier. Bishop and Kasey, you're with me, and squad B. Kasey, you're the only one who has seen Dante. If you make a positive ID, call it."

The rear doors burst open and the tactical teams streamed out. Squad A stormed off to the left, sweeping their way toward the boatsheds. The chief dismounted, carrying his Benelli M4 Tactical Shotgun. Weapon raised, he followed Squad B toward the cafe.

As Kasey stepped out of the truck, the marina's floodlights flickered to life. The whole yard was lit up—including Kasey, the Tactical Squads, and the chief.

They were exposed.

Kasey blinked as she tried to adjust to the sudden light. In the predawn darkness, it was blinding. Kasey felt a hand on her back as she was pushed to the ground.

"Stay down," Bishop shouted.

Bishop's warning was cut short by the staccato sound of automatic weapons being unloaded.

Figures scurried through the cafe's outdoor dining area.

The tactical squad fanned out and returned fire. Their MP5s raised, disciplined bursts cutting through the tables and chairs. Kasey watched as two of the gunmen went down in a hail of firepower. Kasey drew her Glock, but she couldn't get a clean line of sight. The tactical squad was between her and her target. The third gunman flipped over a table and took cover behind it.

Kasey and Bishop clambered to their feet. The tactical squad surged forward, alternating between moving and laying down suppressing fire. The gunman couldn't even raise his weapon without a devastating volley shredding the air around him. He seemed to think better of it and huddled behind the table.

"Advance," the Chief shouted. "The sooner we are out of the open, the better. We'll clear the restaurant first."

Gunfire erupted behind them. Alpha team had run into resistance in the boat sheds.

Bishop appeared behind Kasey. "Let's leave the restaurant to the Tactical Team. We need to clear the offices. Otherwise, our flank will be exposed."

Kasey followed Bishop around the restaurant and found the external door leading into the office block. Bishop tested the door. It didn't budge.

"It's locked. Just give me a minute. I'll pick it," Bishop said.

Kasey shook her head. "No need. How worried are you about the door?"

Bishop raised an eyebrow. "Not at all."

"Good." Kasey summoned her power. "Ehangu"

Arcane energy rippled out from her outstretched hand. The door exploded inward, its hinges twisting and shattering. Bishop blinked, then stormed into the office. Kasey was right behind her.

As they searched the office, its internal door opened. Kasey aimed her weapon in anticipation.

The door swung outward, revealing two armed Bleeding Hearts with their weapons raised. Kasey drew a bead on them. She squeezed the trigger, three times in quick succession. The thug on the left bucked as Kasey's second shot caught him in the chest. His companion raised his weapon, but Bishop was quicker. Two shots later, the thug was on the floor.

Kasey and Bishop crept forward.

Kasey snuck a peek around the door jamb into the adjoining office. The thugs lay still, where they had fallen, but papers blew everywhere. At the other end of the room, an open door led outside. A strong breeze off the Hudson billowed through it, into the office.

"The door is open," Kasey shouted. "Someone else was here too."

"Yeah, but who?" Bishop replied, looking at the thugs on the ground. A pool of blood steadily expanded around them. "These two aren't long for this world."

Bishop grabbed their guns and placed them out of reach of the fallen thugs.

Kasey darted for the door and peered into the night. Two figures ran for the pier. It was difficult to make out their identity in the dark, but the smaller of the two looked like a woman. Her hair flapped in the breeze as she ran. The second figure was much larger.

Could it be Alicia?

As Kasey went to chase after them, the larger figure turned, his face illuminated by the pier's lighting.

Dante Hossack, the bomber who had confronted her at the precinct. The man responsible for blowing up the Langstrode's apartments and rigging Bishop's car to explode. The man responsible for Sal Langstrode's murder.

That must be Alicia with him.

Dante wasn't smiling now. His face was red with rage. He drew a pistol. The light played along the silver of the barrel as he pointed it straight at Kasey.

Kasey's heart pounded and adrenaline coursed through her veins. She raised her Glock and squeezed the trigger, but both shots went wide. She watched as Dante drew a bead on her, his finger tightening on the trigger.

A hand rested on her shoulder. Before she could register what was happening, she was yanked unceremoniously into the office. As she hit the floor, Bishop kicked the door shut.

"What was—" Kasey's question was cut off as bullets tore through the office door. Three deafening gunshots echoed across the marina.

Kasey looked at Bishop who motioned for her to stay down.

"That's a Desert Eagle. Compared to our guns, it's a cannon."

Four more shots slammed into the office, shattering a window and splintering the timber door. Then the pier fell silent.

"Unfortunately for him, it hasn't got much of a magazine," Bishop said, standing. "Let's go."

Kasey scrambled off the floor and threw open the door. Sprinting after the bomber, they ran for the pier. As Kasey cleared the office, she felt a pit in her stomach. Glancing to her right, she noticed a maintenance shack with its windows open.

That's odd. It's too cold for the windows to be left open.

Then Kasey spotted it. Protruding ever so slightly from the window was a blackened barrel.

"Gun!" Kasey shouted as she grabbed Bishop, crash tackling her through the hedge to her left.

Bishop protested as they tumbled through the bushes and rolled free of the garden. Risking a glimpse at the maintenance shed, Kasey searched for a sign of the shooter, only to find the gunmen pivoting toward them.

"Stay down, Kasey. Our vests won't help us against that."

We need more cover. The half-destroyed hedge wasn't going to help their cause. She felt like she was at the Gala Massacre all over again, pinned down by superior firepower. As the thought crossed her mind, she thought of John Ainsley, or more particularly, the spell he had used.

As the gunmen opened up, the bullets from his assault rifle ripped through the hedge, sending leaves and branches splintering everywhere.

Kasey focused her mind on the thug's weapon. "Anghyfiant."

The assault rifle fell silent, its magazine jammed beyond repair.

Bishop stared at Kasey and shook her head. "Where was that before? Why shove me through the bushes when you could have just jammed his gun?"

Kasey shrugged. "That was my first time trying that spell. I didn't want to still be standing in front of him if it failed."

Bishop let out a sigh as she brushed herself off.

"I think the words you are looking for are, thank you," Kasey replied.

The sound of the thug fumbling with the jammed weapon rattled in the distance. Kasey went to raise her weapon and discovered it wasn't there. In the fall, she had lost it. She looked about but couldn't see it.

The tactical team was still tied up in the restaurant behind them. To her left, Dante ran down the pier to where several speedboats were moored. She wanted to go after him but couldn't risk ignoring the thug in the maintenance shack.

"Bishop. Keep your eyes on Dante. I'll deal with our friend and be right with you."

"Right, will do." Bishop clambered to her feet as Kasey sprinted across the exposed yard toward the shack.

The thug's jaw fell open.

Not such a big man without your gun, are you?

She burst through the door of the shack. The thug dropped his now useless rifle and turned on Kasey. As he lumbered toward her, he picked up a hammer from the workbench and brandished it in the air.

Kasey was exhausted. It was past three in the morning, and she had barely had a wink of sleep. Looking at the thug before her, she realized he wasn't in any better condition. His bloodshot eyes watered as he tried to follow her movements.

Scooping a wrench up off the bench, she closed the distance. The hammer came high, a sweeping blow that would have shattered her skull if it connected. Ducking under the blow, she swung the wrench hard.

The heavy wrench connected with his ribs. He let out an involuntary yelp of pain. It was accompanied by the sound of his ribs cracking. As he bought the hammer down again, she grabbed his wrist with both of her hands. He was strong, but she had no intention of fighting fair. As he tried to wrench his hand free, she drove her knee into the his already damaged ribs.

He gasped in pain, letting go of the hammer. She cast the hammer aside before turning on the thug. He was doubled over in pain. Reaching for his neck, she brought her knee up into his face. Years of mixed martial arts had conditioned her for the blow. Her knee connected with his nose. The thug collapsed in a heap, one arm cradling his ribs. His other hand grabbed at his bleeding nose. He wouldn't be going anywhere.

"Stay down and you might survive to see an ambulance. Get up again and the team sweeping the marina will put a bullet in you. Understand?"

He nodded.

She threw the useless assault rifle out the window just in case, and then took off after Bishop.

Bishop was almost at the pier. Unfortunately, Dante had made it to a boat. The engine roared to life.

Kasey watched as Bishop snapped off a few shots at him. The second figure accompanying him was busy untying the speedboat's moorings.

Blinding searchlights illuminated the pier. They were coming from a police vessel that was closing on the marina. Dante ducked, disappearing from sight.

A megaphone crackled to life. "This is the NYPD. Turn off your engine or we will be forced open fire."

Kasey punched the air jubilantly. Dante wasn't going anywhere.

The woman cut the speedboat's ignition, and the boat's engine died.

Kasey ran toward the pier, searching for Dante. Suddenly, the bomber stood up and hefted a large object onto his shoulder. It was cylindrical and almost as long as he was tall. Kasey had seen it in movies, but never in real life. It was an RPG-7 rocket launcher.

She stopped. Her eyes transfixed on the bomber as he squeezed the trigger. A plume of fire burst from the rear of the weapon as the rocket hurtled out over the water. The NYPD patrol vessel was too close. Its captain didn't have a chance to evade the rocket. The rocket-propelled grenade struck the ship and detonated. The white and blue vessel exploded outward as the rocket ignited the ship's fuel tank.

When the smoke cleared only wreckage remained. Fiberglass and shattered debris was strewn along the Hudson. Kasey watched in horror as the two shattered halves of the NYPD vessel slowly sank beneath the water.

CHAPTER 20

K asey was stunned by what she had just witnessed. To make matters worse, the speedboat's ignition roared to life once more. With the patrol boat destroyed, there was nothing between Dante and the freedom of the Hudson River.

Shaking off her shock, she ran for the wharf. Bishop was already on the move. Together, they sprinted for the remaining boats. Bishop looked at Dante's vessel that was quickly disappearing down the river. Without hesitation, she leapt into a sleek powerboat and began casting off its moorings. Kasey reached her just in time and jumped into the boat.

"What are you looking for?" Kasey asked.

"A key for the ignition. We're going after them," Bishop replied. "He tried to kill me. I'm gonna make him wish he succeeded. You cast off, I'll find the key." Bishop began rummaging through the boat.

Kasey threw of the last mooring and looked at Bishop who was still searching for the key.

We don't have time for this.

Kasey rested her hands on the dashboard and whispered, "Dechrau."

The boat roared to life. Bishop stared at her a moment. "I could get used to this."

"It has its perks," Kasey replied with a cheeky grin. "Let her rip."

"With pleasure." Bishop answered letting out the throttle. The nimble powerboat surged forward.

Forcing the boat to its limits, Bishop set out in pursuit of Dante. The sleek vessel skipped over the surface of the water, closing the distance.

Dante looked over his shoulder and for a moment, Kasey locked eyes with the murderous bomber. He motioned for Alicia to take the wheel. Stepping away from the wheel, he fumbled about in the back of the boat, searching for something.

When he stood up, Kasey realized what he'd been doing. Once more he had the RPG-7 rocket launcher in his hands. He'd been busily reloading the weapon. Now it was pointed right at her. Or more specifically, the boat she was standing in.

Alicia let go of the steering wheel and ducked to get clear of the weapon's backblast. The boat slowed but it didn't matter.

"Bishop!" Kasey called.

"I see it," Bishop shouted over the boat's engine. As Dante sighted the weapon on them and squeezed the trigger, Bishop shouted, "Hold on."

Bishop yanked the wheel hard to the left and the speedboat veered wildly off its course. Kasey clung to the handrail to avoid being thrown overboard. She watched in horrified wonder as the rocket-propelled grenade soared through the darkness. It sailed just past them on their starboard side, before slamming into the water. The grenade detonated harmlessly, spewing a geyser of water into the air.

Dante bent down to reload but Bishop wasn't having any of it. "Kasey, take the wheel."

"I can't. I've never driven a boat," Kasey replied.

"Doesn't matter," Bishop shouted as Alicia appeared at the wheel once more. "Just try to keep her steady."

Kasey did her best to hold the powerboat on its current course. She found the bouncing sensation of the boat as it skipped across the water particularly discomforting, but they were gaining fast. Dante's gambit with the RPG had cost them valuable time.

Bishop had other plans. Drawing her Glock, she took a stance and unloaded it at Dante. He ducked for cover. The rounds slammed into the back of the speedboat but made little impact.

Bishop's Glock clicked as its magazine ran dry. Dante must've guessed as much, because moments later, he poked his head up and began reloading the RPG.

Kasey pushed the throttle to the limit. Sixty feet. Fifty feet. Forty feet.

Kasey was closing in.

Dante abandoned the rocket launcher but re-appeared wielding a submachine gun.

Kasey and Bishop ducked for cover. Bullets slammed into the powerboat, shattering its windshield. Kasey crouched lower, letting go of the throttle reflexively.

The speedboat slowed to a crawl as its momentum floundered.

"We can't afford to slow down," Bishop hissed. "They're getting away. If they hit the open water they'll be home free."

Bishop grabbed the wheel and pushed the throttle back to full speed. The speedboat launched forward once more, but they had lost valuable time. The extra space had given Dante the room he needed to reload the RPG once more. He raised it to his shoulder.

Bishop's hands turned white as she gripped the wheel.

Then Dante did something Kasey wasn't expecting. Turning abruptly, he pointed the weapon off the starboard side of his boat.

He isn't aiming at us.

Kasey followed Dante's line of sight. He was aiming at something on the shore.

Her heart sank as she recognized what it was. It was the support structure holding up the George Washington Bridge, the immense double-decker suspension bridge that spanned the Hudson, linking Manhattan and New Jersey. Even at this hour, cars and trucks lumbered across the bridge.

Bishop saw it too. "He's going to blow the bridge. Do something!"

"Like what?" Kasey asked.

"Anything," Bishop replied. "If he blows the bridge, it could kill hundreds of people. Use your magic."

"I don't know who's watching," Kasey replied. "Anyone could see it."

"Then make it subtle," Bishop replied.

Kasey racked her brain, as she searched for a spell that might have the desired effect. She needed something that couldn't be seen.

"Dwynyrawyr!" Kasey shouted as she stretched forth her hand.

It was the same spell she'd used on Brad Tescoe, but this time she made no effort to restrain herself. The water rippled outward as the concussive force surged toward Dante. The wave of energy struck the boat as he pulled the trigger. The boat rocked violently underfoot, and Dante was thrown overboard. The RPG splashed harmlessly into the river.

Alicia screamed, as the speedboat spun wildly. Kasey's spell knocked it hard to starboard. Alicia fought to regain control, but it was too late. The speedboat rammed into the row of concrete pylons that formed a cordon twenty feet shy of the bridge's support structure.

The speedboat exploded as its fuel tanks ignited. What remained of the vessel flipped and showered debris all over the bridge's support structure.

As Kasey and Bishop closed the distance, something emerged in the water before them. It was small, a little bigger than a football bobbing precariously on the water's surface. As they approached, Kasey realized exactly what it was.

"Bishop, that's Dante's head!" Kasey shouted as she grabbed Bishop's shoulder.

Bishop didn't blink. "I know, Kasey."

There was a satisfying thud as the speedboat slammed into Dante at full power.

Kasey winced, then turned and looked behind the boat but couldn't see anything.

Bishop eased the throttle off and brought the boat to a halt. "I think we got him."

Kasey looked at the river. "I think you're right. What about Alicia?"

Bishop studied the flaming wreckage of the speedboat. "There isn't a snowflake's chance in hell she made it off that. Serves her right too, after all she's done. To turn on her own family. It's disgusting."

Something bobbed to the surface of the river. It was a body.

"Hey, Bishop, turn us around."

Bishop turned the wheel and brought the boat around, slowly bringing it up alongside the drifting body. At this distance she could make out the same leather jacket he'd been wearing when he had confronted her earlier.

Sunlight was just beginning to show on the horizon as Kasey reached down into the water. It was freezing. Not particularly surprising for this time of year. Gritting her teeth against the discomfort, Kasey rolled the body over so he was face up.

She pulled him closer and checked for a pulse. There was none.

"What's the verdict?" Bishop asked.

"Very dead," Kasey replied, standing up. "Cold as a slab of ice too."

"And?" Bishop asked. "That water must be freezing."

Kasey shrugged her shoulders. "Yeah, just a little odd, that's all."

"What are you saying?"

"I dunno, Bishop, he should be warmer, he only just fell in the water." Kasey flopped into the speedboat's seat and shrugged. "Don't mind me. It's probably nothing. I'm so tired I can't even stand up. At least we got him."

Bishop pulled the hair back out of her face. "Serves him right. He murdered two dozen people with that bomb."

"Not to mention the Langstrodes," Kasey replied. "Martin, Cynthia, Sal, and, in a way, Alicia. We had almost a week's warning and didn't manage to save any of them."

Bishop shook her head. "Don't be so hard on yourself, Kasey. All that greed, I don't think we could have saved them from themselves."

"Yeah, but with them gone, what will happen to Park Avenue?" Kasey asked. "What will happen to the city?"

"I don't know," Bishop said, collapsing into the other seat.

Kasey let out a sigh. "We may have played right into the Shinigami's hands."

Bishop nodded. "Or we may have scuttled their plan completely."

"How do we tell which?" Kasey asked.

"We're just going to have to wait and see."

Kasey eyed the river. "Should we head back?"

Bishop looked up the river toward Inwood and smiled. "Oh, no Kasey. I'm sure they have everything in hand there. They'll come looking for us soon enough. It's been a long day. Put your feet up and enjoy the view."

As the sun rose, its first golden rays provided a beautiful background for the New York City skyline. Kasey looked out at Manhattan. It was breathtaking. She closed her eyes and sought to summon her gift.

I need to know what's coming.

Channeling her mind, she tried to bring her visions to the forefront of her consciousness while fighting to drive all her other thoughts away. She pictured Park Avenue and focused her entire being on the future she had seen.

Nothing.

Fine. Have it your way.

She opened her eyes to find Bishop smiling at her.

"What's so funny?" Kasey asked.

"You," Bishop said. "We could have died, not once but a handful of times. That's just today. Think about it. Dante is dead. His crew is in custody and we're enjoying a beautiful sunrise. You need to start seeing the glass as half-full, not half-empty."

"I'll see what I can do." Kasey managed a smile, but she was struggling to feel it.

Looking up at the city she loved, she wanted so badly to believe that all was well. Unfortunately, the pit forming in her stomach just wouldn't go away.

When you've seen what the future holds, it's hard to shake the feeling that you already have one foot in the grave.

The End

Kasey might have won the battle but she's losing the war. The Shinigami attack draws nearer by the day, and a fresh murder has set her square in the sights of the Arcane Council. **Curl up with Kasey as she fights for her life in One Foot in the Grave (click here or scan the QR code below)**

Or for the paperback click here, or scan the QR code below.

Looking for more Kasey in your life?

You can join my newsletter here (or click the QR code below). It's where I share my Kasey Chase short stories. You will also be the first to hear about any new releases and giveaways I host.

THANK YOU FOR SHARING THIS ADVENTURE

I hope you had a blast with When Death Knocks. Kasey was the first hero in my Arcanaverse (what we call the universe my books are set in).

As a self-published author, it's just me (a giant introvert), my laptop and a desire to share my stories with the world.

Since I began this journey though, I have discovered I have something far greater on my side. **You. The incredible readers that share my worlds and my love for a good book.**

Like you, I love to read and know you have a never ending To Be Read List. I just wanted to take a minute to thank you for being here with me.

Your support means the world to me, and it makes a difference in helping me bring these adventures to life. Every time you tell a friend about my series or share something about it on social media, it helps me reach readers and share more stories like this with the world.

When you leave honest reviews of my books, it also helps other readers take a chance on me. It is the #1 thing you can do to help me (and Kasey) out.

If you have enjoyed this book, I would love it if you could spend a minute or two to leave a review for me (it can be as short or as long as you like, and the link below will take you to the right page).

Leave a review for When Death Knocks

Thank you, your support makes all the difference!

Until next time.

S. C. Stokes

P.S. I know many readers are hesitant to reach out to an author, fearing that they might get ignored. I am a reader at heart and know how you feel. I respond personally to every Facebook message and every email I receive.
You can find me on:
Facebook
Bookbub
Email: samuel@samuelcstokes.com
You can also visit my website where you can join my newsletter and get a FREE EBOOK and other amazing goodies.

Scroll on for a taste of Conjuring A Coroner 4: One Foot In The Grave

T he Director of the ADI was sitting behind a mahogany desk. His wavy brown hair reached his nape, his messy bangs swept back out of his face. Dark stubble granted the impression of age, though Kasey knew he was the youngest Director the ADI had had in a hundred years. He held a wad of paperwork in one hand, and a cup of coffee in the other.

He startled, then set the coffee down on the table. "Agent Clarke, explain yourself! What is the meaning of this?"

Kasey's gaze fixed on the gun in Agent Clarke's hands.

"Put that thing away and explain yourself at once," Director Sanders snapped, starting to stand.

"Director Sanders," Clarke said, his voice wavering a little, "you're under arrest for the murder of Theodore Getz."

Director Sanders paused, his face beginning to contort with rage. Then, it dispersed, and the Director resumed his calm demeanor.

"Agent Clarke don't be ridiculous," he said evenly. "Whatever you're playing at, it's not funny."

"This is no joke, I assure you," Agent Clarke said. "We have footage of you with the victim yesterday evening. It was taken from the scene of the crime, only hours before he was brutally murdered. We're here to take you into custody."

Sanders shook his head "I don't care what you have. I'm telling you, it wasn't me. Someone is setting me up and I'm not taking the fall for whatever this is." He stood and pointed at the door. "Now get the hell out of my office, while I work out what's going on here."

Clarke held his ground. "I'm afraid I can't do that. I'm here to take you into custody. You can explain yourself to the Council."

Sanders' eyes played across the three ADI agents before him before they fixed on Kasey waiting in the hall behind them.

"You! You did this." Sanders pointed at her, redness coloring his cheeks.

Clarke turned to Kasey. "Why are you still here? Get out of here now!"

The momentary distraction was all Sanders needed.

"Beaduwaepen!" Sanders bellowed.

The magazines fell from the agents' weapons and dropped harmlessly to the carpeted floor. Before her eyes, the guns disassembled themselves, falling apart in the agent's hands.

Clarke raised his hand and shouted, "Heofonfyr!"

At his command, an arc of energy akin to lightning manifested in front of his open palm, before hurtling toward the director.

In the confusion, Kasey didn't hear the counter spell, but the lightning struck the Director's outstretched palm and was simply absorbed harmlessly into his flesh.

Striding forward, Sanders chanted spell after spell, moving his hands like the conductor of an orchestra.

The agent on the left was launched off his feet. He slammed into the ceiling above, rendering him unconscious before he collapsed heavily on Agent Clarke.

Clarke struggled to extricate himself from his colleague.

Sanders turned his attention to the man on his right. The agent was launched back into the hall. He struck the carpet hard before rolling to a stop at Kasey's feet.

Sanders rounded his desk.

Kasey looked between the agents and Sanders. He might be stronger than her, but she couldn't let him get away. The ADI were too busy tripping over themselves to be effectual.

Raising both hands, she chanted "Pêl Tân!"

Two simmering balls of fire coalesced above her hands. Kasey willed them forward. The fire hurtled through the open doorway, sailing straight over Agent Clarke, and bathed Director Sanders in a blazing firestorm.

The director disappeared in the broiling inferno. A moment later, he stepped forward, emerging from the fire unscathed.

One of the globes of fire sloughed off and slammed into the book case. With a roar, the inferno consumed the books before spilling outward. The ruined shelves collapsed, spreading their burning contents onto the carpet.

Kasey watched in horror as the fire continued to spread. Clarke and his fellow agent lay crumpled on the floor, still struggling to shake off the director's assault.

Sanders bore down on Kasey.

"You're behind this, why?" He spoke over the roar of the fire. "Was it simply because I didn't endorse your insane theory when you came before the Council? Now you seek to discredit me?"

Sanders didn't wait for an answer, raising his hands he began to chant. Tendrils of arcane power lashed out from the director. Kasey rushed to erect a shield.

The director's spell manifested his terrible rage. The magic surged toward Kasey, blasting apart the doorway and the surrounding wall. She stumbled backward and landed on the floor. Splintered timber hailed down on her, but her ward deflected the worst of the deadly missiles.

Kasey sucked in a deep breath and rolled onto her face. Her training had served her well. The director would need to do better than that to keep her down.

The director continued his advance, stepping over the crumpled ADI agents.

Clarke shuddered to life. Reaching out, he grabbed the director's ankle, stopping his progress.

Sanders lashed out with his leg, trying to dislodge the agent, but Clarke would not be deterred. Kasey sprang to her feet as

Clarke muttered something under his breath.

A bloodcurdling crack split the air and Sanders' leg twisted at a grotesque angle. He howled in agony. Almost collapsing, he leaned against the shattered remnants of the doorway.

That will slow him down.

Sanders turned his ire on Clarke. Wincing, he raised his palm.

Clarke must have sensed his peril. He bellowed, "Bordrand."

An azure sphere encased him.

Sander's spell struck him a moment later. The azure bubble bent under the onslaught but did not break. A creaking noise filled the air, and the floor began to bow. It gave way under the pressure, the timber splintering like a dry twig as the blast of energy ripped it apart.

Kasey stumbled backwards and fell. She watched aghast as Clarke, his protective ward, and half the office floor, including the other fallen ADI agent, plunged through the gaping hole in the floor.

Sanders gripped the door frame, narrowly avoiding a fall. Catching his balance, he dragged himself to a bench seat outside his office. Placing one hand on either side of the mangled mess, he chanted, "Batian."

A golden light radiated from both palms, bathing his broken leg. Sanders grit his teeth as the bone re-set itself under his magical ministrations. As soon as his leg healed he leapt to his feet. Gingerly, he made his way around the ruined chasm he'd just created and bore down on Kasey.

Kasey's mind raced a million miles an hour as she searched for a spell to slow him.

"Dwrnyrawyr!" Kasey said, sending a dense mass of wintry wind sailing at Sanders like a sledgehammer.

He paused his advance, raising one hand and then the other. Kasey's incantation seemed to slow, then before her eyes it changed course hurtling back at her with breathtaking speed. She didn't get a chance to react before it struck her in the chest, sending her sailing down the corridor.

She slid to a halt. Sanders raced toward her, his face flushed in rage.

"You meddlesome little witch, are you so determined to embarrass the ADI that you would concoct this scheme?"

"What scheme? I had nothing to do with this. I was just doing my job," Kasey said, as Sanders loomed over her. "It's not my fault. You did it!"

"Wyrmgealdor!" Sanders chanted.

A strange sensation wiggled against her back. It scurried along her skin.

She looked down to find the carpet moving of its own accord. The fibers of the coarsely woven carpet snaked around her. Kasey tried to get up, but the serpentine tendrils of the shifting carpet drew her in, steadily encasing her in a tightly woven cocoon. She struggled against her prison but couldn't extricate herself.

She summoned her powers, ready to blast her way out of her imprisonment. Before she could unleash her spell, Sanders loomed over her. Kasey found herself staring up the barrel of his service weapon.

"I wouldn't do that, Miss Chase. My patience is wearing thin. Now tell me why my own agents just tried to arrest me, and why you were with them. The NYPD has no authority here."

Kasey struggled as she spoke. "I'm not here with the NYPD. Agent Clarke dragged me in here when he discovered I was holding evidence from this morning's murder scene."

Sanders nodded. "I see, and which murder scene would that be?"

Sanders' interrogation caught Kasey off guard. As she studied his face, she couldn't tell whether he was simply an exceptional actor or he was genuinely ignorant of what transpired.

How can that be? He was there with Getz.

"I asked you a question, Miss Chase." Sanders clenched his free hand, and the cocoon tightened dramatically. It was growing difficult to breathe.

"Theodore Getz," she said between gasps. "You know, the man you murdered last night."

Sanders shook his head. "I did no such thing."

"Don't lie to me, Sanders. I've seen the footage myself. It's you, clear as day, dragging Getz into the building where we found him in this morning," Kasey replied.

Sanders hunched down over Kasey's squirming frame. "I don't know what you saw, Miss Chase, but rest assured it wasn't me. Theo Getz has been a friend of mine for over a decade. I will find out who did this to him. Whoever killed him is clearly trying to frame me to muddy the waters."

"I saw the video, Sanders, it was you," Kasey said, struggling against her bonds.

"I have no doubt it looked like me, Miss Chase, but magic can do a great many things, including alter one's appearance. Your experience with the Shinigami should have taught you that much. Whoever you saw, it wasn't me." Without waiting for her response, he whispered, "Andwlite."

His form shifted. In seconds, the director of the ADI was gone. In his place stood a woman in a pantsuit, her sandy blonde hair drawn back into a ponytail. The director may have altered his appearance, but his gun remained fixed on Kasey.

"B-but that's illegal," Kasey stammered.

The woman smiled. "So is murder, and I need to get out of here before I face charges for that too."

Sanders used the hilt of his weapon on the fire alarm mounted on the wall. The glass shattered and Sanders reached inside and pulled the lever. Evacuation sirens blared to life.

Sanders holstered his weapon and set off down the corridor.

"Where are you going? Kasey shouted.

"To clear my name," Sanders called over his shoulder, then disappeared into the bullpen.

Kasey lifted her head to look around. Smoke was wafting out of Sanders shattered office. The flames themselves were growing with every passing moment.

"Fire!" Kasey shouted as she looked at the director's office. Her pulse pounded in her ears as she struggled against the enchanted entanglement pinning her to the floor.

The inferno she had started had now consumed the director's office and was rapidly spreading into the hall. The hall she lay trapped in.

She was going to be burned alive by her own blaze.

Join Kasey as she fights for her life, in One Foot In The Grave!

Also By S.C. Stokes

Conjuring A Coroner Series

A Date With Death

Dying To Meet You

Life Is For The Living

When Death Knocks

One Foot In The Grave

One Last Breath

Until My Dying Day

A Taste Of Death

A Brush With Death

A Dance With Death

Urban Arcanology Series

Half-Blood's Hex

Half-Blood's Bargain

Half-Blood's Debt

Half-Blood's Birthright

A Kingdom Divided Series

A Coronation Of Kings

When The Gods War

A Kingdom In Chaos

Made in the USA
Middletown, DE
01 December 2022

16680685R00120